# KILLING TIME

A Short Story Collection

AV IAIN

# Contents

# Iron Thorns

The speakers over my head were close to exploding. They rasped, crackled and hissed like oil tossed over naked flames. It seemed as if the whole room was rumbling. As if a hole would soon open up in the ground.

And I would tumble in.

And tumble down.

All the way to hell.

That was probably the point.

If only Mother could see her daughter now . . .

Gaunt Orb — the band currently on the turntable — were something of an improvement over Hauntlethistle, the previous Album of the Week.

I had that much to be thankful for.

I scanned the shop. It was five minutes from closing time, and there was a single customer remaining. Why did it always have to happen this way?

It was times like these when I would wonder whether Albatross — the manager of Iron Thorns, the heavy-metal record shop where I worked — hadn't made a huge mistake in hiring me — a sixteen-year-old girl on her summer holidays — as a salesperson.

When I'd seen the ad in the window — a week or so ago — I had been hurting for cash pretty badly. The only natural thing to do had been for me to pop in and ask to speak to the manager about the vacancy. I can still remember as — unbrushed long black hair seemingly pouring from every orifice — the man who I would come to know as Albatross slumped out of the back room. He had been wearing a t-shirt with a depiction of a skeleton roaring out of a grave — mud and bone splattering and splintering at all angles.

He had looked me over, creased his forehead, slit his eyes then asked where I wanted to go (the shop was located next to a bus station and it wasn't unusual for lost travellers to pop in looking for directions). When I told him about the ad I had seen in the window, he became even more perplexed. He asked me if I had any previous sales experience.

I told him I didn't.

He asked if I was interested in heavy metal.

*Negative.*

I fully expected him to throw me out on my ear, and to have to turn my job search elsewhere. However, against all odds, he had shrugged then muttered something about starting the next day.

So here I was.

Standing at the till, two minutes from closing.

As I set about counting cash, I inspected the remaining customer surreptitiously, out of the corner of my eye. It was important that I didn't give him any encouragement to approach me directly — I had a fairly firm idea that was what he was plotting. If there was anything I had learned from my week or so working at Iron Thorns, it was that I had suddenly become some sort of demigoddess to all heavy-metal fans who crossed its threshold.

Well, they liked to ask for my phone number, at least.

Given his surroundings, there was nothing out of the ordinary about him wearing a leather trench coat and ankle-high boots. Neither was there anything unusual about the large silver cross he had hanging around his neck.

I glanced over my shoulder, seeing the clock strike five.

I breathed in deep, reached for the volume knob, and faded Gaunt Orb down to nothing. "Uh, excuse me? We're closing?"

The man remained where he was, picking through records. It seemed he hadn't heard me. I have never been the most confident person in the world — whenever teachers pick on me to answer questions in class they are forever asking me to repeat myself.

I gave it another shot.

"We're shutting now?"

Still nothing.

I looked about nervously, hoping against hope that Albatross might emerge from the back room. I knew he would be sound asleep for another hour or so yet. As he had explained to me on the first day at Iron Thorns, he had rather unusual sleeping habits — well, unusual sleeping habits for someone supposedly running a record shop from nine to five, Monday to Saturday. He had informed me that he 'lived for the night' . . . this basically entailed him staying up until ten or eleven in the morning before going to sleep for the majority of the day. I could see why he needed a sales assistant.

"Hey!" I called out.

The man flipped through another couple of records and then turned to look.

Feeling exasperation taking hold, I said, "I'm closing up — you have to leave."

The man blinked to himself several times, muttered something under his breath, replaced the record he had been inspecting, then sauntered off out the door.

I wasted no time in locking up.

With a sigh, I finished counting the day's takings.

---

The following morning — a cup of take-away coffee in my hand — I entered Iron Thorns. Having instinctively gone with black coffee for the first time, I wondered if I wasn't beginning to turn a little metal myself.

As always, Albatross was leaning against the till with his head resting on his folded-up arms — hair all over the place. When I had first seen him like this, I had thought he must be sleeping. After the first time, though, I had realised he was generally receptive to human communication.

I had hardly set my rucksack down when Albatross threw his head back in a storm of hair and roaming eyeballs. He stared at me as if he didn't know who I was, or what I was doing there. As if I wasn't his *employee*.

"He was here — *yesterday* — wasn't he?!"

"Huh?"

"Leather jacket . . . boots . . . green eyes . . . *suspicious-looking*."

I collected myself, setting my cup of coffee down on the counter. "There was someone here till closing, yeah. He . . . he didn't want to leave, actually. He pretended not to hear me." I shrugged. "But he was just looking through records, that's all."

Albatross jerked his head about the room, as if the customer might have been there right now. He looked as if he was ready to fight him. Just what Albatross would look like in any sort of a fight — about the weight of a pro wrestler with none of the muscle — tickled me. "If he comes back here you wake me up, right away. Okay?"

"Okay . . ."

Albatross met my eye, nodding to himself. "You promise?"

"Do you, or do you not, pay me to look over your record shop?"

Albatross gave not the merest glimmer of a smile. "You promise?"

"Yeah, I'll get you if he comes back."

Albatross appeared to be content with my assurances and in due course slouched off to the back room — up to the flat he lived in above the shop.

---

The customer didn't come back that afternoon, and neither did he return the day after. Running a heavy metal record shop proved more boring than I had previously given it credit for. I found myself thinking through all the various scenarios which might link Albatross to the customer who kept on coming to visit.

To begin with, I wondered if they weren't old school friends. And then I entertained myself by imagining that they were former colleagues; working in a supermarket somewhere, getting up to all sorts of hijinks. As I sold a limited-edition pressing of The Burning Blind for an obscene amount of money to a boy not much older than I was, I almost burst out laughing to think that they might have been former lovers.

I did my best to explain this fit of giggles away to the boy retreating with his overpriced vinyl by claiming that I had a cold, but he didn't look too convinced.

It was about five minutes before closing time, when I was going about all the closing-up rituals, and I had turned my mind to planning my evening TV-watching, that I heard the bell over the shop door tinkle into life once more.

When I looked up it was — *sure enough* — the man who had

come in a few days ago. He appeared to be wearing the same clothes.

Leather trench coat.

Ankle-high boots.

Large silver cross hanging down at his chest.

I remembered what Albatross had told me — that I was to wake him from his slumber right away. The thing was — had it been earlier in the day, had I been a touch more awake and alert — that might've seemed like a desirable spectacle. As it was, however, I was mentally prepared to go home. The prospect of staying at work later than entirely necessary — even if it was to watch Albatross duke it out with this leather trench coat-clad gentleman — wasn't all that attractive.

As the man passed by the counter, I raised my voice. "We're just closing up, actually. Maybe come back tomorrow?"

The man made no sign he had heard me. He marched — head down — straight for one of the vinyl racks.

I suppressed a sigh, thought twice about waking Albatross . . . and then — perhaps out of some misplaced sense of female pride — decided I could deal with him without assistance. I approached him. "Excuse me . . . *sir*?"

As ever, the man appeared to exist in a universe entirely of his own creation, flipping through vinyl, occasionally settling on some aspect or other of the artwork.

"Hello?"

Still, the man remained unmoved.

Deciding to press myself more forcibly upon him, I lightly touched him on the arm. This seemed to do the trick. I might as well have shoved a cattle prod down his trousers. He rounded on me, spinning on the spot. I didn't suppose men dressed like this got all that much female contact on a day-to-day basis.

"I need to close up, okay? You need to come back earlier?"

The man eyed me for the longest time. The way he narrowed his gaze was greatly unsettling. It was almost as if he was looking right through me, to something beyond.

Feeling resilient, I took a stronger hold. Although I felt him flinch beneath my touch, he didn't struggle. I led him to the door, then opened it, allowing a gentle breeze in. "I can only bring you this far," I said. "It's up to you now, pal."

The man said nothing by way of reply.

I waited for him to make some sort of movement to leave.

To go back home.

To go back wherever he had *come* from . . .

He took a shuffling step.

And then another.

It was then that I heard his voice for the first time — husky, weak; like that of an elderly man on his deathbed. ". . . Iron Thorns."

"Huh?"

"Iron Thorns."

"Uh, yeah, that's the name of this place." I paused. "You steer clear of here, okay?"

Seeing the man had taken another step, and that he was now out of the door, I gave him a slight push of encouragement. And — just like that — he was outside.

I slammed the door behind him.

---

When I went to work the next day, it was midmorning before Albatross surfaced. This particular morning, he resembled a hairy bush with legs. When Albatross rocked his head back and let loose a rip-roaring howl, the customer I was tending to took one final look at the vinyl he had left on the counter, and which he had been intending to purchase, and set off running. Albatross's howl was so loud and all-consuming, I didn't even hear the *tinkle* of the bell as the door closed on the customer.

For some reason, though, I wasn't intimidated.

I somehow knew it wasn't meant for me.

To tell the truth, I had reached the point where I struggled to take Albatross seriously at all. He resembled an overfed Cousin IT.

When Albatross had finished his hissy fit — or whatever it was he was having — he took several breaths to calm himself down. Then he turned his attention onto me. It took me off guard because from all that had come before, I had expected anger, but there was none. If I had to choose any emotion at all then I would've gone with *fear* . . . he was afraid of . . . *something*.

When he spoke to me, his voice was such a low, defeated growl that I nearly couldn't make out the words. "He was back here again, wasn't he?"

I waited with anticipation, a touch worried that he was going to get angry — that he was going to fire me on the spot. Truth be told, I could really do with *not* losing the job at Iron Thorns. Although a lot of things could be said of Albatross, he was never tardy when it came to paying wages. "Yes," I replied.

Albatross nodded to himself then looked about the shop with frightened eyes. He glanced to me again and then carefully trod his way about the racks holding the records. He paused to inspect a selection. When he was done, he nodded, returned to the counter, a nervous smile on his lips. "No harm done," he muttered, then headed into the back room, from whence he had come.

Before he could totally disappear, however, I decided enough was enough.

"Albatross?"

He stopped dead in his tracks. As if I'd openly and colourfully cursed his mother.

"What is this about? Who is that man?"

Albatross murmured something under his breath.

"Sorry?" I said. "Didn't quite catch that."

Still facing away from me, Albatross bowed his head. I heard him give a heavy sigh. Then he said — at a tone of voice which filled the entire shop, and which would surely have scared away any remaining customers if there had been any — "He has my *soul*!"

After his voice had ceased echoing about the shop, I couldn't help but feel the ripple of embarrassment consume my chest.

Just what was I supposed to say to that?

Thankfully, though, he took the climax of his outburst as an opportunity to elaborate.

Slowly, he turned back to me. He looked thoroughly defeated now. Even though he was a solid two, or three, head-and-shoulders taller than I was, he held himself like a dwarf. "It was years ago," he began. "We had a band together — we were *friends*." He shook his head. "We made some . . . promises . . . *bad* promises."

"And you gave him your soul?"

"Yes."

Knowing that this level of conversation was positively chatty for Albatross, I pressed my advantage. "Why does he keep coming back here? Do you have something he wants?"

His eyes widened out of fear. He glanced over my head, to the shop door.

When I followed his gaze, I saw the man was back again.

The man in the leather trench coat.

With the ankle-high boots.

And the silver cross.

I turned back to Albatross. "Do you want me to lock up?"

Albatross held himself impossibly still. He shook his head. "No. It is time."

We watched the man push his way in through the shop door. He appeared entirely unaware of either my or Albatross's presence there.

We stood watching as the man charted his course through the records, pausing to flip through one or two, here or there. When he stopped at one of the records for a much longer period of time, I heard Albatross take a deep breath, as if in anticipation.

"What now?" I whispered to him.

"We wait."

And so the two of us stood watching the man flip through the records — waiting for something or other to happen. I began to wonder if this was some sort of a joke; and that the two of them were playing it on me . . . just why they might find anything like this funny was beyond me, but, then again, I had never quite got metal at all. So why would I expect to be able to see things from the fans' point of view?

When the man picked up one of the records and turned it over in his hands, Albatross began to tremble. The two of us stood transfixed by the man inspecting the record with apparently minute attention to detail.

And then . . . the man froze.

The way he stood made me think that time had stopped completely. He held the record up to the light, attempting to make out the finer detail of whatever it was he was looking for.

And then he glanced across the shop to where me and Albatross stood.

I half expected him to burst into flame.

But he merely approached.

When he reached us, he laid the record he had selected down on the counter. I looked over the cover, taking in the album art. It was a man — bloodied and naked — caught in a thorny bush. The man was frantically looking back over his shoulder, apparently consumed by the effort of escaping some pursuer. All he was doing, however, was causing the thorns to sink deeper and deeper into his flesh.

When I turned my attention away from the visceral visual, I noticed the lettering at the top:

*IRON THORNS*

Thick thorns sprouted from the surface of the blocky type.

Having given me and Albatross time enough to look over the cover, he turned the record over to show us the other side.

I skimmed the track listing — mainly songs with titles like 'Bane of Blood', 'Cold War Chains' and 'Through the Thorns' — and shifted my attention to where the members of the recording were listed. It was there I saw Albatross's name.

I looked to Albatross, seeing if there was any recognition in his face.

The expression was more like horror.

Deciding I should break the deeply uncomfortable silence which sat on the shop, I asked, "Was this your band? The one you were in together?"

"Yes."

The man was reaching inside his coat for something. From within, he produced a folded-up slip of paper.

Albatross's complexion turned white. He took the paper.

Unfolded it. Shook all over as he examined the note. Then he looked up, nodded.

The man nodded back, then slipped the album off the shop counter, taking it with him as he left. The bell tinkled anticlimactically on his heels.

---

Albatross remained dead still.

I wished myself out of there — somehow . . . but I still had several hours left before I could go home. In the end, Albatross did speak, though it was as much to himself as to me.

"I wanted to produce our own record — I had no money . . . the rest of the band had no money . . . and so . . . and so . . ." He looked off in the direction of the shop door, to indicate the departed man. "He . . . *Michael* . . . agreed to take on the financial burden for the production, but with the agreement that we . . . we gave him our . . . our souls."

I took a moment to reflect on the fact that the name of the mysterious man in the trench coat was Michael, and then moved on.

"He had us all agree, on a piece of paper he kept, that we would grant him our souls." Although Albatross never so much as smiled, let alone laughed, the twisted grimace on his face was the closest to humour I had ever seen in his expression. "We never believed, of course. Never believed in souls. We all agreed." Albatross drew a long, shaking breath. "But we were all so wrong. We made the record, of course, and we had five hundred copies pressed into vinyl. Each band member was given his own copy — from the first five of the run. And that was when the strange happenings started."

"Strange happenings *how*?"

Albatross paused. "We had a short tour lined up . . . in the first show, our bass player was electrocuted on stage so badly he almost died. After a few days, the shock had worn off, and everybody was able to joke about it — to say it was unfortunate. But then, the next night of the tour, as I was singing, walking about the stage, I tripped over my microphone cable and fell off stage. I broke four ribs and needed fifteen stitches in my leg." He breathed in again. "We were forced to cancel more dates, but it was still a joke between us. We thought it was just unfortunate. We laughed about it actually. When I had taken some weeks to heal, we planned another live show. And that was the show when a spotlight fell and killed our drummer."

"*Killed* him?"

Albatross nodded. "Instant death."

The two of us remained silent, out of a sort of reverence, I suppose.

"We cancelled the tour, of course. The funny thing about the whole episode was that all the records sold. They became an instant collector's item. I have seen them in some places going for thousands. My band — Iron Thorns — became something like a legend, or a twisted joke. None of us would make music again."

I waited for as long as I thought prudent, and then stepped in with the first of many questions which swarmed my mind. "You said that something happened to the bass player, and to you, and . . . and your drummer *died* . . . but what about the other members of the band? Were there others?"

"There was a guitarist — and then there was Michael, the keyboard player."

"And nothing ever happened to them on stage?"

Albatross shook his head. "The guitarist — Phil — he

disagreed with selling his soul. Christian, or something. Michael was satisfied to allow Phil to bow out on the condition that the three of us signed our souls to him." Albatross shrugged. "It might have been luck, good or bad, but it might've been . . . something else."

I realised — for the first time since I had started working at Iron Thorns — that there was no music playing over the in-store speakers. "One thing bothers me," I said.

Albatross looked distracted, staring into the middle distance. "Hmm?"

"If that record of yours was worth so much money — if it's truly such a collector's item — then why did you leave a copy of it among the racks, with all the others?"

Albatross remained stone-faced. "I lost my copy years ago, and to my knowledge there was no other copy of the record here at all. Like you say, anybody who had come in here would have spotted it right away, and recognised its value."

"Then, do you think . . ."

"Yes."

"And that — "

"You don't know how many different situations and theories have popped into my head. It cannot be undone." He squeezed the piece of paper Michael had given him into a tight ball then tossed it across the shop. "Whatever the explanation . . . the supernatural . . . *Michael* . . . we are all responsible. All of us who signed away our souls. We are all murderers."

I looked across the shop, to where the balled-up paper had landed. "But why do you think he decided to give you back your soul, after all this time?"

"Who knows?" Albatross replied, heading for the back room. "Perhaps he knows he has got away with it — after all these years. That the blood is dry now. And that his hands are clean. He can just walk away."

When Albatross had disappeared into the back room, I couldn't help indulging my curiosity. I crossed the room to where the ball of paper had landed.

I picked it up and looked at the message within:

*I hereby grant Michael Moorsleigh my mortal soul to possess until the end of all eternity.*

It was signed 'Albatross', and then below, in brackets:

*ALEXANDER LUCAS BAYTRUSS*

Even as I stood there, in the shop, holding the piece of paper in my hand, I couldn't help but wonder — despite the little I knew about contract law — whether or not it made any difference just who was in possession of this note now.

With that thought on my mind I slipped it into my pocket.

Just to keep it safe.

To stop it falling into the wrong hands.

# Shindy

# 1

The air in the stock room smelled of freshly uncanned tennis balls. And it was stuffy as hell. Whenever Allie moved, she felt the sweat dampening the back of her shirt.

There was a deeply annoying buzz coming from the wires which slithered along the stock room walls; wires which she could just about make out in the dim — *surely-not-up-to-health-and-safety-standards* — lighting. Perhaps the world would have mercy on her for once, send her off into the afterlife, or whatever drudgery came next, with a mighty loud *pop* and a shower of sparks.

Whenever she breathed in, she was sure she had overdone her perfume. That thick, honey-scented smell which'd been so at home in wood-panelled courtrooms seemed completely out of place here at Fridges-2-U.

She passed her hand scanner over the bits and bobs — the replacement parts — on the shelves. Even despite everything, she had to admit there was something satisfying about the little *bleep* the machine made when it had successfully scanned an item.

"How's it going, Mrs Hughes?"

An adolescent employee had appeared. He was that lanky blond type with bum fluff sprouting from his chin and upper lip. He, like her, wore the trademark lime-green polo shirt with the jolly caricature of a singing refrigerator — *Freddy Fridge!* — emblazoned on the left breast pocket. He also had a shiny tag pinned to his right breast pocket which read: SUPERVISOR. Despite this lofty assertion, the employee — was 'Joe' his name? — smelled as strongly of marijuana as the rest of the Fridges-2-U staff.

"It's *Ms* actually. But just call me 'Allie', okay?"

Without any discernible expression, Joe clambered up one of the step ladders and pawed at something on one of the shelves. A neat, plastic-wrapped package fell down onto the stockroom floor. He dropped down from the ladder and stooped for it.

The package contained some sort of cable or hose.

Allie waited until his footsteps had completely disappeared, and then dropped her hand scanner on one of the shelves. She stared off along the aisle, past the shelves-upon-shelves of products, all of them in dusty cardboard boxes, kept neat and tidy in well-ordered rows. She wondered if anybody would notice if she stayed here, right on this spot, for the entirety of the day. Thinking back to her own teenage jobs, she recalled how she, and her 'colleagues', would pick out some place at whichever locale they happened to be working: a university library, an ice-cream parlour, once even a go-kart track; and sit about in some sunny spot on a grassy bank and shoot the shit for ten, fifteen minutes. She would return to work with a slight buzz in her chest, knowing she had been Bad.

That she had *slacked off*.

Now, though, she didn't find that same thrill.

She just wanted to get through with her first day at Fridges-2-U and get back home; to her four-bedroom house, where she lived alone, and from which she was expecting to be evicted any day now . . . her first paycheque might just see her through for another month, but only if she implemented her negotiation skills to the very best of her ability.

That was a phone call she *really* wasn't looking forward to . . .

She looked around again, knowing she was well and truly alone. As she picked up her hand scanner once more, she heard something from the shadows of the stock room.

A second passed. Then Allie realised what it was.

*Who* it was.

It was *her* voice.

*Shindy's* voice.

It sent a quiver running across the surface of her skin.

Before she could make sure — before she could be *one-hundred-per-cent* sure — she turned on her heel and left the stock room behind.

To find some company.

So she wouldn't be alone.

## 2

During lunch Allie had gone around the corner, to a nice Italian restaurant. It wasn't until she'd been midway through the set menu — *ricotta with walnut ravioli* — that she'd come to her senses; realised she wasn't a Big Shot Lawyer any longer, and that what had seemed a simple meal would end up costing her half a day's wages.

It had been painful to work through her purse, watching the waiter's card-scanner reject each one of her cards in turn. Finally, though, as if by magic, the very last card in her purse had come good. She had tottered out of the restaurant, glad she'd at least had the presence of mind to wear a jacket, to cover her Fridges-2-U polo shirt. She didn't suppose the restaurant was accustomed to seeing Fridges-2-U employees dining there.

Allie took her afternoon break in the staff room: a windowless place with only an instant coffee machine, a beaten-up table and mismatched chairs, and — inevitably — a fridge. Tomorrow she had to remember to bring in a packed lunch.

With another five minutes of her break to go — and because there was nothing else to do — she poured herself another cup of coffee. To tell the truth, she was hardly in the mood to wake herself up. She preferred being in a dopey state. Working at Fridges-2-U required little more than loping about on customers' heels and reading out the label beside each fridge which listed capacity, energy saving, and lifespan . . . because the task of reading seemed to be beyond most customers. As she had been reminded to do several times over by Joe, she made sure to emphasise the extended warrantee: 'no-hassle returns' for any fridge that didn't meet the customer's high standards.

She was sat at the table, alone with a sad trickle of coffee in her mug, when she heard voices out in the hallway. Thirty seconds later, Joe and another young male employee — *all* the employees were young and male — came caterwauling in through the door. Once the two of them had given Allie a quick once-over, they stopped laughing.

Allie glanced at her watch, then turned her attention back down to her coffee cup.

"How you getting on?" Joe said, taking a seat opposite, a glass of milk before him.

Allie did her best to raise a smile.

There was no reason why she couldn't be *friendly*.

"Oh, fine," she lied.

The two boys promptly removed their mobile phones from their pockets and plonked them on the table. After a couple of taps on the screens — and apparently finding no urgent missives waiting — they turned their attention back to the real world, to the staff room.

Joe glanced to his companion — a boy with gelled black hair and a clunky keychain dangling from his belt strap. Taking a sip of milk, Joe jerked his thumb in the black-haired boy's direction. "This's Marko — only been here a week." Joe placed his milk down on the table. He had given himself a milk moustache. "Before you came, he was the newbie."

"The new-what?" Allie put in, not really thinking, feeling a little *floaty*.

Joe's phone buzzed. He grabbed for it, tapping away frantically at the screen with practised skill. "*Newbie*," Joe replied, half-distracted by his phone. "New-blood, new-around town." He smiled a little wider.

From his easy manner, Allie could tell Joe thought quite a lot of himself.

Had being a SUPERVISOR gone to his head?

"So I'm the *newbie* now?"

"Uh huh," Joe said, taking another swig of milk and then slamming the glass back down. It made a loud *thunk.*

Allie flinched.

Arms folded on the table, phone abandoned for the time being, Marko leaned toward her. He looked like one of those types who had a perpetually running nose. He also squinted as if he might need glasses. "Ainchoo a bit *old*?" he asked.

Allie was taken aback. She missed a breath. ". . . Pardon me?"

Marko slipped Joe a glance.

Joe stared at his phone, either not listening or doing a good impression of someone who wasn't listening. Being a SUPERVISOR, Allie supposed Joe might have an inkling of where the law stood on age discrimination in the workplace.

"You're like the same age as my mum, shouldn't you be at a real job?"

Allie slipped Joe another glance, as if he was going to put his neck out for a 'newbie' . . . especially one who was old enough to be his mother.

She felt her throat close up, but she forced herself to meet Marko's eye.

He had inky, *black* eyes.

As if he didn't have any irises at all.

"I lost my real job," Allie replied, speaking to her coffee cup.

When she glanced up, Marko and Joe were staring at her.

At least she could tell Joe was listening now.

She supposed she owed them *some* explanation.

The interview had been conducted by Sepp — the owner of Fridges-2-U — but, as he had stated when he'd offered her the position, he was away on business this week.

Joe was in charge.

Joe clearly hadn't had the opportunity to peruse her CV and she wondered if Marko knew how to read at all . . .

No, these two hadn't seen all those years of work as a lawyer — all those years of law school — which she had felt were superfluous to her application even as she'd been jotting them down on the form. And yet, she hadn't wanted to lie. She had seen no point in *lying*.

She was *proud* of what she had achieved.

. . . No matter where it had brought her.

"Well," she continued, realising she couldn't stop now, "I was a lawyer — I used to stand up in court, defend people."

"Yeah, yeah," Marko said, rolling his eyes, "we might work for Fridges-2-U but we're not *idiots*, all right?"

"Right," Allie replied, and then glanced to the fridge as if it was a monolith.

"What happened, then?" Marko asked, still with his hands propping him up on the table, and staring at her with those eerie eyes.

"I . . . well, had a . . . an *episode.*"

"What's that?" Marko said. "Something like TV? Were you on one of those shows they do about idiot people? You know, when they have some investigator, or summink, showing up people what's incompetent?"

She was amazed Marko had a word like 'incompetent' in his vocabulary.

She glanced back at Joe, as if he might put this conversation out of its misery. But Joe was back to staring at his phone. She looked to Marko. "It's sort of where you lose the plot — when you forget what's real, and what's . . . not."

There was a long silence and then Marko shook his head. "Ain't got no idea what you're talking about, lady. You'll have to be more specific."

"A break-up, that was what triggered it."

Here, apparently out of nowhere, a smile snuck up on her. The smile developed into a chuckle. She brought her hands up to her mouth, to shield her lips. She straightened out her expression. "It's a silly thing, really. Just something from my childhood."

"What?" Marko asked, leaning closer.

"Well," Allie replied, "when I was a little girl, I lived in a big house with my parents — this *huge* house out in the countryside." She paused for a moment, feeling giddy, and then a touch nauseous. "The only problem was that I'd get *so* lonely. It was in the days before all the entertainment we have now. The only thing we had was books. This was before the internet."

"So what'd you do?"

"Well, I used my imagination. *A lot.* I pictured things that weren't there."

"And what's it got to do with your 'episode' ?"

"I invented this person — a *princess.*"

Marko snorted a laugh. "Ain't people like you supposed to be in the nuthouse — to be afraid of the men in white coats?"

Allie, though, was unperturbed. "I used to call her Shindy."

## 3

Thirty years ago, Allie had felt the sweet, warm wind up against her cheeks. The gentle breeze blowing through the leaves. She pressed her back up against the thick, rough bark of her favourite tree: an oak tree at the bottom of her family's apple orchard. She would come here whenever she saw Shindy. That was best.

This way, she wouldn't get into trouble.

She was *always* getting into trouble when she was alone.

Allie could still taste the thick, heavy-on-the-batter brownies which their housekeeper — Mrs Gregory — had prepared earlier that morning. The taste mingled with the scent from the apple trees, creating an almost irresistible mixture in her mind.

What she wouldn't do for some friends.

Something or *someone* to keep her mind occupied!

A red squirrel hopped into view, just a few paces in front of her. It gripped an acorn firmly in its teeth.

Out of nowhere, a foot came down on top of it.

And crushed it into the ground with a stomach-turning *crunch.*

She felt as if all the air had left her lungs. Her heart beat hard in her throat. She looked up, to the perpetrator, although she was sure — *already* — who it was.

Golden curls.

Rosy-red cheeks.

A pink, frilly tutu.

Shindy.

Allie turned her attention to Shindy's black pumps, to the bloody mess.

"Oops," Shindy said, with a slight smile, wiping her shoe in the long grass.

All at once Allie felt a rage building inside. She curled her fingers into fists. She wanted to beat Shindy to death for what she'd done . . . and yet, something held her back.

Allie knew she was incapable of harm, that she didn't have a mean bone in her body.

At least that was what her mother was always saying . . .

Feeling her throat tightening, she looked up at Shindy. "Why?"

Shindy finished wiping her sole and gave a light-hearted shrug, avoiding eye contact. "Come on," she said. "Let's go *play.*"

Allie stared long and hard back at Shindy, and then she looked back up to the house, to the way back through the apple orchard. She sunk her teeth into her lower lip until she tasted blood. And she tried her best — *really she did!* — to shake her head.

But it was impossible.

No matter how much she wished it wasn't so, Shindy was a part of her.

*Forever.*

# 4

On the bus back home from Fridges-2-U, Allie pressed her forehead up against the chilled glass. It was getting on for that time of year again — *autumn* — and soon the long warm days would be replaced by freezing-cold mornings and early-arriving nights.

And all while she continued to work at Fridges-2-U.

At some point, the heaters kicked in on the bus, and Allie felt the warmth suckling at her skin, bringing out that worn-down, sweet smell of sweat. All that time on her feet throughout the day reeling through the merits and pitfalls of freezer drawers, interior plastic racks and energy efficiency savings versus cooling power . . . among other things.

Her mind felt as if it was ebbing apart, like an iceberg slowly breaking up and floating away. She wondered how much longer she could take it.

How much more of this could she put up with?

When she got back home, she wasn't in the mood to make anything substantial for dinner. When there was no one to share meals with cooking was a real chore. She had never married — she wasn't the *type* — but she had had a long-term, live-in boyfriend called George. That was the break-up she had mentioned to Joe and Marko today.

But, like everybody else in her life, it seemed, he had deserted her.

Left her alone.

She flipped the kitchen radio to one of the talk channels. That made her feel somewhat less alone. But she knew it wouldn't be enough.

She listened to the presenters drone on and on about the economy.

In the end, she got herself out of her work clothes, peeled off the Fridges-2-U polo shirt and dumped it in the hall. She put on a grey-blue tracksuit; the one she used for jogging; the jogs which she had cherished before a frantic day in court. She never listened to music. She enjoyed the silence — the signs of the waking world around her.

And Shindy hated jogging.

So Allie *was* always alone.

She couldn't go jogging now, though. Not unless she wanted to return home to a cold shower and a dark, lonely house. Hot water and electricity had been elevated to luxuries in her current situation.

Shivering, she put a thick jumper on over her tracksuit top. That done, she poured some cereal into a bowl. The fridge wasn't working so she hadn't bought any milk. She leaned against the kitchen counter as she crunched her dry cereal. Even though she wore thick socks, she still felt the chill of the laminate tiles.

When she'd finished eating, she dumped the bowl in the kitchen sink. As she looked through the window, into the back garden, she saw her reflection. And then . . .

*Shindy.*

In the reflection, Allie saw Shindy standing behind her, against the wall. Her golden curls hung in ringlets. Her rosy-red cheeks that'd never known rouge. And the pink, frilly tutu she wore. Last of all, the sparkly, silver tiara perched in her hair. The one which — back when Allie had been a little girl — Shindy had purloined from her mother's bedroom. Allie had been severely punished for both the theft of the tiara and the dead squirrel which her mother found in her underwear drawer.

As Allie took in Shindy's beaming, pearl-white smile, she tried to see into the depths of her soul. Where had she come from?

But all Allie knew was she'd come back.

# 5

Six months before, Allie had been hurrying about her bedroom.

Just like always, she multitasked: keeping everything compartmentalised in a different section of her brain. She jabbed in her earrings, slipped on her shoes. Spoke rapid-fire into her mobile phone, crooked between ear and shoulder, blabbing away to her legal secretary, Laura. Simultaneously, Allie did a mental inventory of her briefcase, of all the papers she needed that day.

It was a big one — child custody.

Emotions running high.

Both parents in court.

She would need to be at her most professional.

With the strong taste of mint ebbing through her mouth, she breathed in her wonderful honey-scented perfume — the perfume which she often thought of as softening her appearance, making her seem a touch more feminine than her fiercely ironed trouser suit would suggest. At least to those who got close enough to smell.

As she bounded out through the bedroom door, she caught her shin on the wooden edge. Just as she had learned from her upbringing, she said nothing at all, only hissing air through her teeth in frustration. Just like her mother used to do.

She flew down the stairs two at a time, only stopping when she reached the front door. She rested her fingers on the latch. Felt its familiar weight beneath her touch.

*Suitcases.*

Three of them.

She stopped dead. Glanced up.

*George.*

He stood in the kitchen doorway. A dour expression on his face.

"Please," she said, "can we talk about it when I get home?"

He remained silent.

She *had* to go . . . no two ways about it.

She would arrive late for court otherwise.

Which, perhaps, in retrospect, might've been for the best.

She had done her best to black out the day in court. But she could remember the shenanigans only too clearly:

Shindy queuing up to enter the courtroom.

And then — with the case proceeding — how Shindy had flown out of her seat.

Grabbed the judge by the lapels.

*Screamed* in his face.

And how police officers had dragged her away.

Allie.

*Shindy.*

. . . *Allie.*

*Both* of them.

# 6

The next day at Fridges-2-U, Allie woke at half past six, took a cold shower, dressed, then caught the bus. She was first to arrive, and she found herself standing at the door until about fifteen minutes past the scheduled opening time. She supposed the manager being away meant Joe and co were taking liberties; no doubt having a puff on the 'Magic Dragon' — or whatever was the modern-day parlance — before coming to work.

When Joe *did* show up, he was dressed in black jeans with a puffer jacket over the top of his polo shirt. He had deep, black circles beneath his eyes. He didn't vocalise any sort of greeting, only giving her an indifferent nod as he dug about in his pocket for the keys.

That morning, Allie surprised herself. Somehow, from somewhere, she plucked up a happy demeanour. And customers reciprocated her smile. Before she had really got a handle on what was happening, she had sold three fridges: two of them to couples, and the final one to a — *rather-fetching* — man about her own age.

He was the opposite of George. Whereas George was skinny as a beanpole, this man, was broad-chested, muscular. And he had bright red hair and pale skin, whereas George had been well tanned and had dark-brown, bushy hair.

As the red-haired man attempted to fathom the card-scanner she noticed he was shaking. "Can I help, sir?" she asked, her voice much firmer than she had planned.

The man glanced up, met her eye for a second, and then quickly shook his head.

This time he managed to work the machine. He gave her his address for the delivery and she handed him the receipt.

He promptly left.

The man had been gone five minutes when Joe appeared at her side. He kept his voice to a drawl. "Listen," he said, "I don't know much about romance, but I'm fairly certain he's interested in you." He paused. "You single?"

Unable to think up a suitable response, she just blabbed, " 'Alone' ? Yes."

# 7

Allie noticed a certain tightening-of-the-ship when Sepp — the owner-manager — returned. No longer did Joe — *and Marko* — show up reeking of marijuana. And they always arrived on time. But not before Allie.

As Allie worked away at Fridges-2-U, she couldn't help but notice the hostility, bubbling just below the surface with Joe. A couple of times, as she just happened to be passing by, while he was seeing to some customers, she overheard him incorrectly describe a fridge's specs. When she butted in, politely but firmly, to correct him, she thought she could feel the burn from his scowl all the way to the back of her skull.

The resentment took a more direct form during one of the afternoon coffee breaks.

Like always, Joe had a glass of milk. He would intermittently take sips while tapping away at his phone. They never spoke now — there wasn't even the day-to-day politeness of greetings any longer. That was okay with her, though. With Shindy's help she picked out a book to take along to work each morning.

On one of these afternoon breaks — when Joe had left his phone behind to briefly slip out and go to the toilet — she had caught a glance of the screen:

Joe: Man, u hear anything 'bout that warehouse job?

Marko: Nah, soz.

Joe: Cant see myself taking it much longer. Not with Ms Bitch bout the place. Shell be after my job soon dont u rekon?

Marko: Its alrite, bet them men in white coats'll be in 4 her soon.

Joe: Yeh, theres always that I guess.

Allie heard the toilet flush. She teared herself away from the mobile phone screen before Joe retook his seat at the table.

# 8

The next day, early in the morning, Sepp called Allie into his office.

Marko and Joe were there too. She couldn't help wondering if they'd maybe made up some sort of infraction in the hope of getting her fired.

So that Joe could save his arse.

However, Sepp — as ever looking disorganised with the papers cluttering his desk, and smelling strongly of body odour covered by deodorant — dug out a tablet computer from the top drawer, tapped away at it and then handed it over to Allie. "Order. Remember the customer? One of yours." He then made an odd gesture, fluttering his hand about his head, which Allie deduced — though not after a decent amount of effort — meant *red* hair.

The nervous red-haired gentleman from before.

"Right," Allie said, feeling her chest tighten.

Sepp nodded to Marko and Joe. "You two go with her — to do the heavy lifting."

As she left the office behind, the tablet computer tight in her grasp, she felt almost as if she could cook an egg with the searing-hot gaze she got off Marko and Joe.

She watched on as Marko and Joe lugged the fridge up into the back of a white van — with that same caricature of Freddy Fridge doing a merry jig emblazoned onto one side. She wondered how long it would be before Sepp thought of *officially* replacing Joe with *her* as supervisor. Because she was already the de facto supervisor now.

Joe drove the van with Marko sandwiched in the middle. Allie peered out the window, watching the blurry landscape passing by. They reached the customer's house, way out in the countryside, in about twenty minutes.

As Joe and Marko unloaded the fridge, Allie paced up the gravel path to the semi-detached house. It had a thatched roof and an overgrown garden, bushes growing so thickly that they almost covered the windows. She rapped on the brass door-knocker and waited.

When the red-haired man appeared in the doorway, huge and muscular and — beyond his freckles — flushing deeply, Allie greeted him with a smile, asked him to sign for the delivery. He was shaking. He could hardly sign his name straight.

Perhaps Joe had been onto something when he'd said that he liked her.

A broken clock told the right time twice a day after all.

"Thanks," Allie said, turning away.

She waited for him to say something. For him to tell her to wait . . . for him to maybe ask for her number . . . but then she saw he was distracted by what played out before them.

Neither Marko or Joe was lugging the fridge along.

Both of them wore a white coat.

They marched toward her.

Stiff, deadly serious expressions on their faces.

From somewhere, Joe had produced a straitjacket.

Before she could say anything at all, they grabbed her:

Marko on one side, Joe on the other.

She was powerless to stop them as they thrust the straitjacket down over her head.

Her vision blurred.

Freddy Fridge — on the side of the van — leaped about.

And then . . . right when she was ready to give up, she felt

Marko and Joe's hold on her slip. With a final effort, she thrust herself away from them and fell.

In the near distance, she heard Joe's voice — raised in protest.

"Get your hands off me! We've been sent here to *section* her!"

"You're a meddling little *gobshite*!" a voice replied.

. . . The red-headed man.

No longer was he timid, hanging back. Now he was grappling with Marko and Joe — and their *white coats* — wrestling them back into the van.

With a *roar* of the engine — and the *screech* of tyres — Allie felt herself being lifted upward, in a firm, unbreakable grasp. She looked into the red-headed man's eyes and saw a look of extreme concern. "Are you okay?" he asked.

He spoke with a thick Irish accent.

Her throat felt tight and she could only nod.

"What was that about . . . ?" he began.

But before she could answer, Allie fell into his arms.

## 9

Marko and Joe weren't fired.

There was no need.

They never returned to Fridges-2-U.

And Allie saw no point in telling Sepp just what had happened, either. He seemed to have so much to be getting on with as it was — and Allie was pleased enough with her promotion to SUPERVISOR. Taking Joe's place.

Marko and Joe's little scheme — their *prank* — to have Allie lose her mind, run off and leave them be, had well and truly backfired.

In short order, she lost her home — there was nothing she could do to save it with the earnings she had from Fridges-2-U. However, after several weeks of courting, she moved in with the Irish customer — Padraig. He seemed to lose his nervous tendencies soon enough.

Although Padraig never pressed her to explain the intricacies of the 'prank' which Marko and Joe played on her the day at his house, she decided, eventually, that he needed to know. That he needed to know about *that* portion of her life.

That he needed to know about *Shindy*.

She thought he might leave her right away, that he might believe her to be some sort of a nutcase . . . like anybody in their *right* mind might.

However, he understood her.

The first person in her life who *tried* to understand her loneliness.

And he seemed — *mostly* — to get it.

Padraig was appalled at what had gone on. Once he found

out the details of the 'prank,' he seemed all ready to go out, track down the boys, and bring them to 'justice' . . .

But Allie held him back.

She told him she wanted to leave things be.

That it had been like a bookend for that period of her life.

Because now things were looking much better.

Soon enough, she might fight her way back into her career.

It didn't matter what people said.

*Somebody* out there was bound to employ her.

*Somebody* wouldn't have heard of That Day in court.

It was that very evening, as Allie rose from the bed she shared with Padraig — to fetch a glass of water — that she caught herself taking a glance in the hallway mirror. And there looking back at her was Shindy.

Shindy was smiling and waving . . . waving *goodbye*?

Allie stood her ground until Shindy had disappeared.

She looked herself in the eye.

And smiled.

# The Just War

When Clive Hopper woke feeling his septuagenarian's chest filling with fluid, it was all he could do to cough it away, turn on his side, and go back to sleep.

It had been like this for so long now.

That bitter, bloody taste of phlegm at the back of his throat.

The unshakeable, cotton wool-like numb sensation in his skull.

And, over everything else, that smell of earth.

*Everywhere.*

It didn't matter if it was spring, or summer, or autumn, or — like it was now — *Christmas*.

These dreams visited upon him every single night.

He would've thought that he might've grown accustomed to their horrors, to the ever-widening black pits, devoid of sensation or warmth or life; all these images which plagued his subconscious mind. But, no.

*Cough*

*Cough-cough.*

*Cough.*

And then Clive would have opened up an airway, enough so that he might be able to breathe. Enough so that he wouldn't suffocate in his sleep.

Some nights he wondered if that would be a bad thing.

Some nights he didn't just wonder.

Clive had always hated the winter — had hated the way that his dust allergies, given a reprieve in the autumn, were handed a fresh kicking by the central heating. And he hated the most how he couldn't go outdoors without bundling himself up in half a dozen layers.

Just so he wouldn't *die.*

The one thing that gave him pleasure in the cold, distant, winter months — aside from the hope that he might slip away to death in his sleep — was the cooperative effort he had going with some other old folks who lived on his estate. Together they'd all pitched in — granted some with more grumbles than others, but they'd *all* pitched in — and together they'd bought up just about every tacky piece of Christmas tat they could get their hands on. And gone and plonked the whole collection at the end of the estate, on Constance Green's front lawn. They had hooked it up to Constance's electrical systems, and they had all agreed to pitch in with the running costs of such a wondrous spectacle.

Oh, it was actually pretty glorious, now Clive allowed *that* particular thought to dwell in his mind.

Glorious in the way that it was a bit of fun, and that it was hurting the square root of *nobody*. He recalled when they had gone down the garden centre, and how he'd noticed the shop assistants, so diligently helping them out, nudging and winking between themselves as if it was the funniest sight in the world to see a gaggle of old codgers buying up Christmas tat. But Clive hadn't paid them any mind.

He knew from experience that he and young people just came at life from totally opposing angles . . . as if they'd been born on other planets.

Clive could recall the little display the garden centre had set out front. How there'd been those light-up 'Christmas' animals: reindeer, turkeys . . . beavers? . . . had that been what they were? In any case, it hadn't mattered, because, with their combined savings and assorted vouchers, they had bought them all up. And then they'd moved onto the Father Christmases, and their sleighs.

*Cough . . . cough . . . cough . . .*

Clive turned on his side. With a crooked eye, he examined his bedside digital alarm clock with its slightly nuclear, red LED display.

It had just gone half five in the morning.

That was enough . . . enough sleep for one night.

He hoiked himself out of bed, dumping his duvet on the floor as if he was a child. He supposed that if his mother had still been alive — by some freak of spirits, or science, or a little of both — she might've chided him for it. Clive had never got married so once she was gone he hadn't had anyone left to tell him what to do.

How to behave.

Clive shuffled into his slippers.

It was only as he got out onto the landing, as he approached the long glass window which peered out into the street, that he realised there was something Not Quite Right.

His window peered out into the estate. It looked all the way along the road, and to the end of the street. He could see that neat, *tacky* display that he and his aged brethren had erected. As he squinted, he realised there was a large car plonked at the end of the street. He could see it, even in the half-light from the orange streetlamps.

A pair of figures — dressed in black — were moving among the display.

Clive watched on as one of the figures grabbed a glowing reindeer: lit with a series of white and yellow lights. The lights blinked a few times. And then they went out.

They loaded the reindeer into the back of the car.

Clive furrowed his brow.

He recalled the day they'd set out the display; how their mouths had been *stitched open* with laughter. There'd been long, rambling discussions about where to set up the nativity scene — that had come from the garden centre too — and then there had been further arguments about where exactly they should place Father Christmas with his glowing sleigh of reindeer, all set to ride off into the Nether.

It had been a good day.

A *memorable* day.

Strange to think that it had happened only a week ago.

It felt almost like a lifetime.

Clive was quick down the stairs. He was out of the door almost as fast.

He glared at the *burglars.*

"Oi!" he called out.

Although Clive struggled for breath on the best of days — not to mention nights — he found he still had a hypnotically strong *bark* on him. He could send shivers down someone's spine if he so wished.

The burglars turned to him.

The one lugging an illuminated beaver promptly dropped it, rushed for the car. The beaver hit the lawn, bounced a couple of times, then its lights went out.

Clive trod onto his front lawn. He fixed the two burglars with a searing stare but could do nothing save watch them into the car.

He listened to the *rattle* and *hum* of the engine as they took off.

The early-morning breeze chilled his exposed calves.

He didn't dare take in the dilapidated scene.

The wreckage.

---

Clive acted as soon as he felt it polite to make phone calls. The first person he called — at seven thirty — was, of course, Constance Green. Thankfully, she hadn't heard anything that morning, and she hadn't yet thought to look out into the street.

He quietly broke the news, told her, in straight, plain facts, just what had gone on, and what he planned to do about it. Most important of all, though, he informed her that she should simply sit tight and await further instruction.

That was pretty much the key to all management.

Let people know — in easy-to-understand terms — exactly what was expected of them. Maybe he should write a book. Nah, he was *too old* to write a book — and it would be a pity if he died before he could finish it . . .

Next along, he phoned up Jack Stephens.

Good Old Jack.

Jack lived across the road from Constance, and — Clive could *bet* — he had witnessed just about every single moment of the robbery. Despite being a veritable curtain-twitcher, Jack never acted on anything he saw. Clive had only to mention the burglary and Jack revealed he had indeed seen all, and furthermore he had taken extensive notes — with *timestamps* — which they could, theoretically, hand over to the police when the time was right. As always with these moments, Clive decided against scolding Jack for not having opened up that *famous* window of his and having shouted something at the pair of burglars while there was still time to stop them. The saying 'can't teach an old dog new tricks' seemed to carry a certain truth to it.

Or maybe Clive had just got *lazy* in his winter years.

Clive's final call was to Graham Kingsley.

Graham didn't live on their street, but he had helped to put up the display. Like Clive, he was disturbed about what had gone on. Unlike Clive, Graham had a cabinet full of rifles, and — again *unlike* Clive — Graham was all in favour of swift and thoughtless vengeance . . . indeed, Clive was near enough certain that, any day of the week, any hour of the day, Graham was angling for *vengeance* of some kind. This, though, this went *beyond* vengeance.

This was a Point of Order.

Once Clive had got off the phone with the other three oldies, he made himself a large pot of coffee and — during the course of the morning — drank his way through it while he did the newspaper crossword.

---

At precisely ten thirty — crossword finished; fully showered and dressed — Clive yanked on one of his thick winter jackets, double locked his front door and then set off to the rendezvous point:

Constance Green's front lawn.

The others were already there.

Graham and Jack had made good progress in terms of putting the display back together. Clive couldn't help but notice the burglars' efforts had been mainly focused on the glowing aspects . . . on the Father Christmas, and the reindeer, the *beavers* . . .

They'd left, arguably, the most tasteful part of the display alone: the nativity scene.

Clive looked to Constance who stood up on her front doorstep, arms folded over her chest, shaking her head, pinching her lower lip with her teeth. When he drew closer, he realised she was mumbling beneath her breath.

"You know, talking to yourself is the first sign of madness," Clive said.

"Hmm?"

Clive looked Constance over. It was funny how it worked. He found himself, so often whenever he looked at someone his age, thinking about how they might've looked much younger. How they might've looked when they'd been in their *youth.*

He supposed others looked at him and thought the same.

Clive examined Constance, took in her purple-blue hair, the peachy tone of her skin. Clive knew, from his experience of women, that she must put a good deal of expensive lotion on her skin every day. He wondered about that.

Did she think she could recover her youth?

Did she think that — *one morning* — she might wake up and find herself back in that twenty-something's body?

Didn't Clive think that?

Today Constance wore a knitted pink scarf wrapped tight to her throat. Clive could see that she was shivering slightly and — thinking on his feet — asked that she go inside to make some tea. With a smile, Constance acquiesced.

Clive went over to check up on Jack and Graham. The two of them stood with their hands on their hips admiring their work. They had picked the Father Christmas up off the lawn and rearranged the reindeers.

Clive glanced at the all-weather, multi-power outlet they'd picked up from the garden centre. And he couldn't help but stare at the empty socket. Where the purloined reindeer had once been. He shook his head. "What'd you reckon it was about?" he said.

"Bastards," Graham said, shaking his head. "Just *bastards*, that's all."

Jack had a slightly more constructive contribution to the discourse. "They were old," Jack said. "Not as old as us, but — you know — they weren't a pair of teenagers."

"No," Clive agreed, "I saw the car from my doorstep — not the sort of thing some teenager could afford . . . or borrow without their parents noticing."

"Definitely not teenagers," Jack said, and then jerked his thumb over his shoulder, in the direction of his house, across the street. "Got it all in my notebook — I can go fetch it if you like."

Clive shook his head. "Nah, it's all right, don't think we'll need it for now."

Graham scratched at the back of his neck, and Clive heard the vaguely disgusting sound of dead skin becoming caught beneath his fingernails. "You reckon it was some kind of scavenger hunt? You know, one of them high-spirited things where they have to go get a bunch of unrelated stuff. Maybe they had to tick a light-up reindeer off their list?"

Again, and it seemed like he was really making a habit of it now, Clive shook his head. "Not likely, I'd say. Too old, for one thing."

"Yeah," Jack put in, "guys like that, you would've thought they'd have families at home, wouldn't you?"

And it was right then, as he heard Constance calling them into the kitchen for tea, that Clive felt the penny drop.

*That was it.*

---

Clive kept to himself throughout the following hours, but he made sure that his determination was plain for all the others to see.

He wasn't having this.

Not again.

And — he was *certain* — they would return tonight.

The burglars.

Graham was extremely glad when Clive asked whether he could meet him after dark at Jack's house with a couple of air rifles. It didn't seem to matter *too much* to Graham that it wasn't a *real* rifle. Any excuse to shoot something seemed to raise his spirits.

When they did meet at Jack's house, with Constance and Graham there, as agreed, there was a spot of confusion about what they were to do next.

Clive cleared it up for them in no time.

"We're going to wait," he said. "Wait till they come back."

Throughout the waiting hours, to while away the time, they got out the dominoes, and then, when everybody decided that they were *bored* of dominoes, they whipped out the bridge table and had a game. All the time, they didn't close the curtain to the window in Jack's front room.

They needed a clear view out into the street.

It wasn't until about three a.m. that Clive heard the familiar *rumble* of the engine.

The car.

Back again.

The burglars.

The others had drifted off to sleep in varying poses.

Jack in his armchair.

Graham splayed out on the sofa.

Constance sat upright at the other end of the sofa, blanket drawn up to her chin, head tilted back. Snoring away.

Clive smiled to himself.

He grabbed one of the air rifles.

Put on his winter jacket.

He roused the others, instructed Graham to come along with him, since he couldn't quite count on Jack being anything else than a burden. One thing was for certain, if Clive put so much as an air rifle in Jack's mitts then he would never — *not in a thousand years* — think to shoot it. Even if given the order in unpleasant terms.

Clive left Constance behind to take care of Jack.

He didn't want Jack to get to feeling that he was intentionally being left out.

Clive wasn't in the business of bruising *anybody's* ego . . . least of all his own.

That was why these burglars had to go down.

---

Clive and Graham snuck on out of Jack's house through the French doors around back. They skulked their way along the side passage, both of them with their air rifles clasped in their grip. When Clive dared a look back at Graham, he saw that he had a smile smeared all across his face. He knew Graham could hardly believe his luck.

As they came around the house, into the front garden, Clive saw that — just like the night before — the car had pulled up on the road.

The two doors opened.

The burglars, familiar from the night before, alighted.

Clive signalled for Graham to hold back, and he really *did* have to signal. Clive was concerned that if he *didn't* give Graham some input he might shoot first and aim later.

And Clive wanted to keep Graham nice and manageable.

That would be the only way he'd be useful to him.

The burglars blended in nicely with the shadows which surrounded Constance's front lawn, and Clive observed as they kept themselves in the darkness. He supposed they were taking no chances; knowing that old fogies tended to be light sleepers.

They might — just as easily — be awake right now.

Ears perked up to hear any sound.

What these burglars were doing was *cruel*, Clive reflected, because the reason they came during the night was so that they wouldn't be discovered by those *younger* neighbours, the ones more likely to be able to do them some sort of harm.

More able to stand up to them.

Well, Clive and Graham were about to show them the error of their ways.

Clive could feel Graham's hot breath on his neck.

It was almost as if he was with a dog, raring to get at a rabbit crossing a field.

But Clive had to hold him back.

*Not yet . . . not yet . . . NOW!*

Clive blustered out from his cover, hearing the *stamp* of Graham's army-issue boots at his heels. He raised his air rifle up and shot off several times.

Graham did the same.

Both burglars went to ground.

Both let out loud exclamations of surprise.

And more than one swearword.

"Stay down!" Clive shouted out to them as he crossed the street.

He kept one of the burglars, the one now lying on the lawn beside Father Christmas, within his sights. Out of the corner of his eye, Clive could tell that Graham was, silently, taking charge of the other burglar. That he was approaching him with his own air rifle outstretched, ready to fire at a moment's notice.

As Clive approached the burglar cowering on the lawn, he caught a glance of the pink collar of the shirt he wore beneath his black robe, or *whatever* it was.

The burglar was wearing a balaclava, and he seemed to be trembling.

When Clive stood over him, pointing his air rifle at the burglar's chest, the burglar said, in a voice that sounded a lot like a spoiled eight-year-old, "You *shot* me!"

Clive rolled his eyes. "It was only a BB."

"A 'bee-bee' ? " the burglar replied, as if he hadn't understood.

"Take your headgear off."

As if the burglar had forgotten he was wearing anything at all, he reached up to his head. Padded at the balaclava a good dozen or so times, apparently attempting to find how he might pull it off.

*Finally* he succeeded.

Clive stared down on his prisoner.

When he glanced back at Graham, he saw that he had achieved the same feat with his own hostage. Now they had the two of them. Both of the men, without a doubt, even with Clive's slightly squiffy eyesight, and the poor lighting here, were in their forties. They both had tubby beer guts and were balding . . . still at that stage of life where they were clinging to the last bits of fluff that stuck to their scalps. My oh my, how Clive could remember *that* stage. He even reached up and ran his hand over the stubble of his bald head as some kind of nostalgic gesture.

Both men looked positively terrified.

"What'd you think you're doing tonight, huh?" Clive said, putting the question to his hostage.

His hostage — the man in the pink shirt who looked like he might be on the verge of tears — said, "We . . . we . . ." but he couldn't get out any more words.

His associate picked up the slack in the interrogation.

"It was our *wives*," he said, his tone of voice sounding as pathetic as his excuse.

"Your '*wives*' ? "

This time Clive's hostage managed to speak up. "Yes. Our *wives*."

Clive shook his head. He glanced back over his shoulder, ostensibly to Jack's house, to see Jack and Constance's faces beaming out at him, but, instead, he realised that he and Graham had somehow managed to raise the whole street.

All the houses had lights on.

A couple of people were standing on their doorsteps.

Looking out to see what was going on.

Clive guessed he'd better cut to the quick. "What'd you mean your *wives* made you do this?"

This time it was Graham's hostage who spoke up. "An eyesore," he said. "They think it's an eyesore."

"And how's that?" Clive said, with a slight grin, thinking that — *just perhaps* — these men's wives had taste after all.

"Well," Graham's hostage went on, "we live back there" — he pointed off across the road, to the new housing development; the one with the wrought, iron cast fences, and the well-tended flowerbeds. "Those lights, they're there whenever we look out the windows, at night."

Clive exchanged glances with Graham, and Clive could tell that they were *both* doing their best not to crack up. Oh, sure, the police might be on the way. As far as Clive and Graham knew, they might be set to spend a night in the cells. But this whole . . . *situation* was just *too* funny. These two middle-aged men quivering away. Pushing their wives out as their excuse.

Clive inspected the men a little closer, and then said, "So, you thought the solution to the problem would be to *steal* our little display here?"

The *impromptu* burglars exchanged glances, and then Graham's hostage replied, "Yes, that seemed the best way to do it."

Clive stared back into the eyes of Graham's hostage, wondering just how much he should enjoy himself. In the end, though, he decided he should just settle on the truth. Oftentimes there was no point in muddying the waters just for the sake of muddying them. He puffed out his chest, and said, "What we've got here is just a little bit of fun — some Festive Cheer — you know that, by January, it'll all be gone." He drew in a breath, realised there seemed to be more and more people standing out on their doorsteps. He noticed both Constance and Jack were standing on Jack's doorstep looking out too.

Clive turned his attention back to the men, both of them now looking thoroughly ashamed of themselves . . . as they well might. "You mean to tell me — to tell *us* — that you couldn't put up with a little fun for just a little slice of the year. Allow yourself to be just a touch uncomfortable for a short time?"

Clive needed no answer to *that* question.

It had been rhetorical.

"No," Clive went on, "I can see what this is about, more than these Christmas decorations, the matter goes further than that." He glared at the two men, as if he might be about to fire off a couple of fresh shots with his air rifle. "You don't want us here — *in your neighbourhood* — in the neighbourhood of the Young, of the Families, because, surely, all we Old Folks do is get all uppity, bringing our set ways down on you lot like a ton of bricks."

Clive felt his chest heaving a little. More of that fluid filling his lungs. He wondered if he might need an ambulance. But if he made some murmur about it now, it would completely defeat the gravity he had managed to construct.

"You're disappointed," Clive continued, "disappointed that we stayed — that we didn't ship ourselves off to some home, put ourselves out of the way, so we no longer need to be looked at."

The two men's ashamed looks were all the answer Clive required.

With a slight nod to Graham, Clive headed back across the street.

To Jack and Constance, waiting there on the doorstep.

What a night.

---

The following night, Clive stood up on his landing, looking out through the long glass window, into the street. He could see the merry glow of the reindeers, and the Father Christmas — in his sleigh . . . even those beavers seemed to be pulsating some sort of cheer.

He breathed in deeply, and then sighed out.

The fluid in the lungs had been a false alarm.

Another one.

He was still here, *pinned* to this world for at least another few hours, another few days, months . . . years?

As Clive looked along the street to where they'd re-erected the display, he noticed the car pull up at the curb.

Tonight, though, there was no sense of immediacy, no signs of do-or-die about it.

Because there would be *no* operation tonight.

With only the gentle clicking *purr* of his own breathing to provide a soundtrack, Clive peered out through the glass to the family getting out of the car.

He watched one of the men — the one who'd worn the pink shirt the night before — go around the back of the car and extract a purloined reindeer. With a pair of children — one girl, one boy — watching on, he replaced the reindeer where it had once been. He turned his back, apparently finished, but then right at the last, with a knowing glance from his wife, he returned to the reindeer.

Crouched down.

Plugged it into its socket.

And the reindeer glowed away in the darkness.

Just a little Christmas cheer.

Clive smiled.

# The Hairbrush

The hairbrush sat on the edge of the dresser, on its back, its reflection caught in the mirror. Its bristles were stiff and made of the finest black horse hair. The handle from well-polished bone which shone a dull, jaundice-yellow in the evening gloom. Before the hairbrush, the couple bickered, throwing up their hands, arms flailing, fingers like nobbled twigs. A perfume bottle smashed up against the wall and its glass tinkled down. The pungent grassy scent pattered down on the hairbrush, soaking into its bristles, seeping into its bone.

One of the couple caught the hairbrush with their elbow, sending it tumbling down where it fell into the bushy carpet, its bristles splaying as it landed, bent outward at all angles. Lying there in the carpet, the perfume scent grew irrepressible and the bickering of the couple reached a fever pitch.

In the flash of a knife the argument ended once and for all.

The hairbrush just lay there.

The grass-scented perfume thickened in the air and mixed with the heady, rusty stench of copper. A slick crimson puddle lapped at the handle of the hairbrush.

---

Weeks and weeks passed by and the room filled with other odours, but the hairbrush remained in its place. Its bristles grew surer in their new position, less and less likely to ever move out of their mould. The perfume seeped deeper into the hairbrush, becoming more and more inextricably one with it.

And then everything happened quickly.

The hairbrush lay where it had laid for so long, so that it now seemed out of place to be anywhere else. There was the trudge of boots up the stairs, the mumbling voices in the hall, and then the gentle *creak* as the door to the bedroom opened wide.

The hairbrush just lay where it was, still splayed and seeped in the stenches of the room, bristles crushed forever more. First they came for the body, and then the people dressed in white suits, masks over their faces, entered the place. Their search was thorough, all-encompassing. But they almost missed the hairbrush.

Gloved fingers closed around the handle of the hairbrush and a virgin, resealable plastic bag opened with a slick tear. And the hand dropped the hairbrush into the cold, smooth bag and sealed it up. The hairbrush remained where it was, a museum exhibit, trapped there within the bag. And then it was dropped into a squidgy case, as white as the people's suits.

Then all went black.

---

Fluorescent lights blinked on around the hairbrush, and a latex-gloved hand reached down, removed plastic bags with other relics swiped from the couples' bedroom: a nail file, a bag containing fragments from the smashed perfume bottle, and then something which didn't belong in the bedroom at all: a long-bladed kitchen knife matted with dried blood.

That same hand brought the hairbrush up too.

The gloved hands swiped a cotton bud against the hairbrush, and then unweaved a few strands of hair from its crushed bristles.

Soon enough the gloved hands replaced the hairbrush in its plastic bag, stuck on a sticker which had the number seven printed on in a thick red font.

---

When the light returned to the hairbrush, it found itself sitting on a table, before a courtroom, dozens of faces staring down on it as it was scrutinised, prodded and held up. All still inside its clear plastic bag. And, on its way back to the bag, to re-join all the other plastic bags, the other objects, one of the couple stared down at the hairbrush as if it had damned them to hell.

But all the hairbrush had done was witness.

---

It must've been months, perhaps a year or more passed, when the light arrived again, and the hairbrush was relieved of its plastic bag. It was carried in a heavily-calloused hand, past several grim faces, down a corridor of barred prison cells, further on and on, the footsteps steady as a metronome.

And then, after a pregnant pause, through the door and into the cell at the end of the corridor. One of the couple stood staring out through the letterbox-sized window, barred, out into the gloomy afternoon, arms folded on the windowsill.

The calloused hand passed the brush over, and then one of the couple turned the hairbrush over to read the gold-plated inscription in the handle, still made half-obscure with the dried blood sticking to it:

To Katherine,
With all my love,
Drew

# Brought Back Blood

That Friday night blood was the last thing on my mind.

The Pistols were in town, but that wasn't where we were headed. This mate of Thommy's told us where we could check out something more authentic. This band called Three Blind Dykes. Three women, obviously, or some blokes in drag . . . after about half a dozen pills I don't think anybody could rightly tell the difference.

At least I couldn't.

It was dribbling rotten piss. I could feel it trickling down the collar of my jacket, drooling down the back of my shirt. Filthy water got in through the hole in my left shoe, making my whole sock sopping wet. I could feel a cold coming on, that sort of blocked feeling at the back of my throat. That feeling which wouldn't let the beer go down so nicely.

The place was a broken-down town hall called *Twin Turns* at Hodge Hill, Birmingham.

Inside was the kind of wet heat you get from people who've slogged long and hard through a working week and then got a good drenching out in the English fog and rain for their trouble. But they were putting paid to those woes in the form of beer and all kinds else. As was I.

The house lights were up and there was a Pistols tune playing over the PA, I forget which one. My head was stuck in a funk already, by then. Truth be told, I was thinking long and hard about slogging it back through the wind and rain and fog to my dumpy, draughty bedsit back across town.

On windy nights — nights like this — the windowpanes would rattle in their frames.

On stage, a pair of guys in black shirts, black jeans, who might've been anywhere between thirty and fifty, were lugging gear back and forth.

The career criminal in me couldn't help but note those long moments when neither one of them was keeping an eye on the amplifiers, or one of the guitars. It wouldn't take much effort to nab something, and, from what I could remember, the bouncer on the door wasn't anything much that a size eleven to the forehead wouldn't take care of.

I knew better then, of course; that it'd be more trouble than it was worth to get the stuff fenced, to actually feel the cash in my back pocket. I was closing on the age where I was actually beginning to appreciate that old adage 'crime doesn't pay' . . . or — at the very least — I was starting to catch a clue that crime, when not done properly, can get you into all sorts of bad shit.

I shrugged the shoulders of my trench coat, padded my breast pocket for some fags, but found nothing. I vaguely remembered firing up the last one, then tossing the packet into a gutter streaming with rain water. The fag had made my head feel like it was swelling up so I'd tossed it after only a couple of puffs. Remembering that swelling feeling made my hands stop shaking just a little. My heart stopped its constant jigging.

No fags, not till later.

Thommy and that aforementioned mate of his were coming back from the bar, loaded down with pints spewing sallow foam over the rim. "Here you go, pal," Thommy said, passing over mine.

I took my glass from him, supped at the head of it.

Sour.

An unpleasant taste of disinfectant.

Still sent a warm ooze through my blood, though.

What I most remember about Thommy's mate was how he had his blue jeans hitched up over his belly button. How he had every last button of his white shirt done up, all the way to his collar.

First time I laid eyes on him, I thought him a funny fucker, like he was some wannabe yuppie; the kind that'd begrudgingly thought he should go some way to achieving it, without *actually* achieving it. He had the shirt, he had the smartish appearance . . . but he was lacking in the details.

The jeans, for one, made him look scruffy, and, for two, his blond hair had obviously never seen a comb. Much less any sort of product.

When he stood, he would invariably tuck one of his hands into the back pocket of his jeans. Even then, holding a beer, he tucked the unoccupied hand into his back pocket.

I knew that there was something in there.

That he had *something* that was giving him some sort of comfort . . . like a kiddy squeezing a teddy bear to their chest, or some shit.

I have to be honest, when I heard later that one of the Three Blind Dykes had got her face cut up, I thought only of Thommy's friend.

Thommy's friend was the first who came to mind.

---

The support for the Dykes was a Beatles tribute act.

Their manager had picked the wrong show — the wrong *crowd* — that much was for certain. They were promptly sent skittering for the side of the stage within the first minute of 'I want to hold your hand'. As for myself, I caught Ringo a good one with my tossed pint glass. I'd only drunk it halfway down, but it seemed the appropriate thing to do.

With the fake Fab Four having been sent scarpering, some student in thick glasses with a microphone showed up on the stage and mumbled something about something before getting himself clocked with a boot in the forehead. He went off rubbing at the affliction and the Dykes showed up in short order.

When they started to play, I couldn't help noticing Thommy's mate getting riled by something or other. It was like watching him go through his entire life in single moments: excitement, ecstasy, despair, loathing . . . and all the time reaching for the back pocket of his jeans, unable to leave alone whatever he had concealed there.

As I sipped at my drink, I made a point to keep my eye on him. If there's one thing that getting stabbed'll teach you, it's that you don't want to have it happen again.

Not to *you*, in any case.

Thommy's never had the best taste in mates — and I'll be honest and say I'm probably not the exception to that particular rule. The way Thommy works, he collects strays; all those who sit on the fringes, in the gaps; neither this or that.

And, I suppose, in that way, Thommy's mate fit the type.

Still, the way, through the whole of the Dykes set, that Thommy's mate was fishing about in his back pocket made me think that he was going to pull a knife. That he was going to flip out. You can never predict what somebody's going to do once they've got alcohol, or otherwise, in their system.

As the Dykes rained down their own brand of merry hell upon the room, I tried my best to catch Thommy's eye, but he was having none of it. And I soon caught onto the idea that he was doing his best to avoid me; that he didn't *want* to speak to me.

Well, *fuck him*, since he was the one who'd invited me out here.

Once the show was over, I stretched my mind to think of anything out of the ordinary, anything more out of the ordinary than Thommy's mate himself. But there was nothing which I could make out. Nothing which struck me as *distinctly* odd . . . perhaps there was something I was refusing to see . . . something which I was wilfully hiding from myself.

Yeah, or maybe — *just maybe* — I was getting played.

Because when we hit a bar nearby later, a pair of coppers came in asking after everybody's names and details and made a beeline for me.

Almost as if I'd been pointed out to them.

The one that'd cut up the Dyke's face.

---

Of course they had no evidence. Just some people who said they'd seen *me* sneaking about backstage. It'd been at that point, near the end of the show, when I'd got myself separated from Thommy and his mate, so there was — *conveniently* — no witness to corroborate my story; to confirm or deny where I was, or wasn't.

When everybody's conspiring against you, it can seem like you're the crazy one . . . that *you're* the deluded one who, for whatever reason, just refuses to see the truth.

Staring back at them out of the gloom.

But I know, for myself, that I was nowhere near backstage, and I told the police as much. Being someone with a 'profile' doesn't help matters much. It's not like there's anything in my past to contradict the story being built up around me.

The only reason I got off at all was because the Dyke who got her face cut up couldn't pick me out in an identity parade. And there was no wonder because she had, most likely, never seen me in all her life.

The police gave up on the case soon afterwards. I guess that they didn't much care for dealing with the seedy underbelly of the punk scene. They thought we were all rats and they wanted us done with. If we ripped one another apart then so much the better.

Although the scene might've looked chaotic to those on the outside, to those who weren't *part* of it, there was definite structure; which was to say that you were in, or you were out. And the one guy who stuck in my mind from that night as being 'out' was Thommy's mate.

Maybe those police didn't think enough of us punks to get their hands dirty and *do their job*, but I had a little spare time, and a lot of inclination, to go about clearing my name.

So that was what I did.

I decided to go see the Dyke first, seeing as the police seemed done with her and my involvement. She lived in a block of flats not too far away from *Twin Turns*, one of those sixties concrete monstrosities as Britain struggled to come to grips with the Baby Boomers spewing forth from every womb:

North, west, south, east, and much of it landing in the midlands.

As with all those places, it stank of piss and cigarettes, though I didn't much mind either. I'd carved out a career of such places and if you were to honestly ask me what I smelled, I'd probably tell you that it was money.

She lived in a place on the fifth floor, and the only way I knew I'd found the right place was because it was the only apartment which didn't have a numbered plaque . . . or, at least, it was the only number that somebody'd made off with.

Two firm knocks later, and I found myself staring back into a single eye, peering out at me through the crack in the door; the chain very much engaged.

"What?" said the voice from inside, a woman's voice, short and stubby, and, no doubt, used to having to shrug off male attention.

Namely women I'd been around my whole life.

"Shawna live here?"

The woman's eye narrowed. "Who wants to know?"

"Roger," I said. "Roger Peterson."

I waited to see if there'd be any sort of recognition on her part . . . I knew the police hadn't dished out names but information has a habit of leaking.

"Roger Peterson!" the woman barked into the flat.

I waited, glanced either way, along the exposed corridor, to the faraway drop behind me. This wasn't the sort of place you'd like to bring up kids, but I could see a couple of small bikes left haphazard at the end of the stairs.

Kids should've taken more care if they didn't want them nicking.

From within the flat, I heard low-level mumbling.

The eye appeared in the gap again. "All right," she said. "Come in."

---

I've always been pretty aware of my appearance, of how a six-foot-five, bald-headed guy in his forties, who near always dresses in a trench coat and ankle-high boots, meets most people's expectation of 'threatening'.

Not so on the scene, where someone like me is the norm.

An outcast.

Not that I ever tried to be anything else.

It's the ones who're trying to be someone else you've got to watch for.

They're the threatening ones.

The room smelled thickly of dust and damp. Smoke rose up from some unseen ashtray and the TV was idling in the corner. There was a slumped-over form in an armchair. I could tell that the form was staring at me through dozy eyelids. When I took another step forward, I realised that the dozy eyelids were really bruises. It was tough to tell in the dim light of the sitting room, but the bruises looked pretty bad.

"Luce?" the slumped-over form said, in a weak, brittle voice.

The eye which'd peered out at me in the corridor appeared in a doorway.

I hadn't realised she'd slipped away.

"The lights?" the slumped-over form said, finally.

With a near imperceptible sigh, the eye — Luce . . . Lucy? — flipped a switch. Near-blinding light filled the room, chasing all the shadows into the corners.

I turned back to the slumped-over form, the Dyke I'd come to see.

I took in the bright-red lines, running on both her cheeks, around her mouth.

Down her neck.

It made me wince just to look at her.

As with everything in the scene, you hear stories, you hear about the horrors second-hand, but there's something about being up close and personal, actually *bearing witness*, that just can't be communicated through talk or song.

She looked like she'd been beaten up, all right.

Beaten up *bad*.

The Dyke straightened up, better bringing her injuries to bear in the light, and then gestured to the armchair alongside.

I glanced around, saw the eye which'd met me at the door had slipped on out again.

I crouched, perched on the arm of the chair for a few moments, then thought better of it and sank into the cushion. With my height, it's better to get low on people as soon as possible; part of the whole not-being-threatening thing.

"I'm Nathalie," she said, finally. "At the door, that was my sister."

Transfixed by her injuries, it took me another few seconds before I noticed she was holding out her hand to me. I gave her hand a shake. "Roger," I said.

"Yeah," she replied, with a raspy voice. "I heard, from the door."

For some reason, I felt a shade nervous.

I drew in a deep breath.

Looked to the TV — some news report.

"Not many people have come," she said.

"What?"

"At first," she went on, "when I got out of hospital, every day somebody would come; with flowers, or chocolates, or . . . whatever . . ."

She nodded in the direction of the door. There was a table covered in bouquets of dying flowers, unopened boxes of chocolates.

I turned back to her, with a slight smile and a shake of the head. "Not very rock 'n' roll," I said.

She snorted. "Nah, not really my thing, either."

Once the two of us had smiled about this detail for a couple of moments, Nathalie returned her gaze to me. I knew that she was testing me with her injuries, seeing how I would react to the scars and bruises. I would be lying if I said that they didn't faze me, but, at the same time, I'd seen worse.

I'd seen bone sticking up through torn flesh.

I'd seen eyeballs dangling out of sockets.

I'd seen *bodies*.

But, from her face, I could see that she'd been beautiful — she *still was* beautiful . . . and once the swelling went down, I hoped that she'd recover some of her former self.

"You've come about the attack, haven't you?" she said.

Seeing no reason to lie, I nodded.

"Who are you, Roger?"

I told her — about being in the identity parade, about how they thought I'd been the one to do it.

She pouted. "Thought you looked familiar — thought I'd seen you before."

"Yeah," I replied, "lots of people say that — sometimes I think it's because of my size; it's difficult for me to go unnoticed." I gave a shrug. "Probably what happened that night, huh? Somebody probably just remembered me?"

"Maybe," she said.

I thought about the times when I'd been turned down for good-paying jobs because of my height — because whoever was running the job was concerned that I'd be too easily pointed out later on . . . that I'd compromise the whole operation.

Sometimes I wonder what my life might've been like if I'd

come in at around five foot ten or eleven . . . would I have been a master criminal if not for those extra inches?

Nathalie sniffed, then looked away.

I suppose I should've asked her sister, Sarah, if it was appropriate for me to ask questions about the attack. It wasn't like I'd wanted to set off any painful recollections . . . but, then again, why'd I even gone there in the first place?

I pressed on, deciding this should be like picking a scab.

*Quick and painful.*

"I wanna find out who did it."

"Who did what?" she shot back. "Oh," she went on, reaching up for her face, "*that.*"

"Think I've got an idea."

Her eyes met mine — *blazing*. "Do you?"

"Are there any details?" I said. "Anything that sticks out in your mind? Anything you didn't tell the police?"

Nathalie was in the middle of shaking her head.

Then she stopped.

She stared me straight between the eyes.

"There was one thing," she said.

---

At least the attack hadn't stopped the music.

On my way out of the flat she shared with her sister, Nathalie handed me a freshly pressed 45" of Three Blind Dykes' latest single. The entire sleeve was black with a single scrap of paper stapled to it written out in a near-illegible, cursive script. The single was called 'Brought Back Blood' and she said that they'd played the song at the show.

To be honest, I couldn't immediately bring it to mind.

But I would put the song on later.

I headed on down, and to Thommy's house in Hall Green, on the other side of town.

There was never any point in knocking on Thommy's front door, so I just wandered in, almost being knocked over by the stench of marijuana smoke wafting about within. I padded the breast pocket of my trench coat again, found the pack of cigarettes, slipped it out. I'd always hated that over-sweet, rotten-fruit smell of marijuana, though I'd always hated its effects more. It made a man soft; it made him let his guard down. It wasn't anything like alcohol or cocaine which got him firing on all cylinders.

But each to his own.

As I prodded the cigarette in through my lips, lighting it from a match, I took in the pair of younger boys in Thommy's kitchen. Both of them were in a daze. Both of them with a spliff squeezed between their fingers. Dead to the world.

I trudged on by them, out into the garden then to the shed where I located Thommy, lying on a mattress he had stowed there. He had on a scrubby shirt over a pair of stone-washed jeans. Everything about him looked filthy. He was leafing through some book while he had the radio on loud and distorted.

That was one of Thommy's weird protests, how he would go on all day about how the radio just played dirge. He'd switch it over onto some commercial channel and play it loud, so loud that the sound distorted, so that hardly anything could be made out except for the *buzz* of the plastic casing.

When I asked him about it one day, he told me he did it to make the music more 'real'.

Thommy was that sort of guy.

"That mate of yours," I said. "The one who was at the Three Blind Dykes show?"

Thommy continued to flip through pages.

I gave him a kick with the toe of my boot.

He flinched, glanced up at me.

His mouth peeled in a wry smile.

"Rodge," he said. "How've you been?" He reached up, scratched at his skull the same way a mechanic might dig about in his toolkit for the right spanner. "My mate?" he said. "The one who went to the Three Blind Dykes show?"

I waited patiently, not wanting to rush him.

When Thommy willed it, he could slip into a wickedly uncooperative mood.

Uncooperative wouldn't help me.

I wanted justice.

As the Three Blind Dykes might've put it, I wanted to 'Bring Back Blood'.

"Shit show, that?" Thommy said, allowing his book to fall open to his current page on his chest.

I made no comment — knowing that this observation was mostly rhetorical; a way for Thommy to dig through his addled memory; to find something concrete to tie the recollection in with.

Thommy laid his tongue on his lower lip. "That'd have been Charles, I'd think."

"Charles?"

Thommy gave a brisk nod, blinked a couple of times, and then returned to his book, as if he'd forgotten I was even there at all.

God damn that funky herb . . .

I lurched forwards, grabbed hold of Thommy by the neck of

his shirt, and dragged him up. This didn't quite have the effect I was hoping for; he only grinned sheepishly at me.

"Listen, all right?" I said, feeling the heat on my own breath. "That girl, the one from Three Blind Dykes, she got cut up pretty good, and I'd like to find out who it was that done it. I've a good mind that it's your mate . . ."

I paused, waiting for him to fill in.

"Charles," he responded. "*Charlie.*"

*Charles*, I thought to myself. *Fucking Charlie.*

Fucking yuppies.

"Where's he live?" I said. "Where can I get a hold of him?"

Thommy picked this particular moment to smooth that smile off his lips, and to meet my eye with a steely glare. "What beef've you got with Charlie?"

I gave Thommy a shake. "They took *me* in for it, you know — the fucking police. They thought that *I* did it."

Thommy flashed a grin. "Looking to clean your good name?"

"Something like that."

"Well, then," Thommy said, glancing at where I held him.

I let go of him.

It wasn't like he had anywhere to run.

"Think I can help you out, pal — I mean, if that's what you want."

I watched Thommy stumble about his shed, searching for a pen. When he eventually turned up a pen but couldn't find paper anywhere, he tore out a page from his book.

Wrote out the address across the lines of text.

"Here you go, mate. Take care, won't you?"

I took the paper from him.

Glanced at what was written there.

Then, with a nod, I slipped out.

---

This bloke, Charles — *Charlie* — lived in and around the centre of the city.

It wasn't too much of a challenge to track him down to one of these new housing developments; an up-built complex which'd be the wet dream of just about any Young Urban Professional. A fucking yuppie like *Charles*.

There was this turnstile system I didn't fully understand, so I hopped over it.

Inside the complex, there was a whole bunch of saplings; the tobacco-coloured soil had been recently stirred up to plant this, that or the other.

The address Thommy had written out for me was for a flat going by the name of 5F.

I tracked it down.

Then rang the bell.

A sharp *buzz* sounded within the place.

I slumped back on my heels.

Waited.

And waited . . .

It was then that I wondered if Charles would be at work, if he'd be hitching up his yuppie trousers, clasping his yuppie briefcase, and hitting it down to his yuppie office with his yuppie pals. Maybe I could come back later.

Night-time would probably work to my benefit.

Just as I was preparing to turn myself around and to come back later, I heard some scuffling around the back of the flat. I glanced to the side of the place, realising that there was a side alley I hadn't previously seen. I looked about, seeing if anyone was around, and, realising there wasn't, I ventured in through the gap.

Again, because of my size, I'm somewhat wary about being seen sneaking around places — I stick in the mind and I tend to be a dependable motivation for people to break free of their inaction; to make them pick up the phone.

Dial the police.

Still, I thought myself in the clear, and went around the flat.

Found myself facing off with a garden gate that came up to just below my belt buckle.

I stepped over it.

Into Charles's garden.

There were baby bushes sprouting all over the place, and a gravel pathway that was already strewn with weeds. It looked like these places always did about six months after they'd been handed over from the construction company to the fledgling owners; ones who hadn't ever owned a property before . . . not that I'm one to judge — I've been a renter my entire life.

I glanced about the garden, waiting for reason or rhyme, and it was then that I noticed the dog — this Spaniel-type thing — disappear through a large flap in the exterior door.

Again, I looked around, and hoped nobody was watching.

I got the door open by sticking my hand through the flap, grasping hold of the key within. I slipped in and brought the door shut behind me. When I stood there, in the middle of Charles's kitchen, I was struck by the cleanliness; everything fucking spick-and-span. It seemed to me that this Charles bloke had a cleaner . . . either that or he was several shades of obsessive when it came to looking after his pad. Maybe it was just simple yuppie pride.

The dog sniffed about my boots, but thought better of giving me a bite or a bark.

I trod about the kitchen, orientating myself, putting myself in Charles's shoes, trying to think through what a yuppie like himself might do.

I pawed through the drawers, looking for I don't know what . . . until I found what it was that I didn't even know what I'd been looking for.

Nestled there.

Inside the drawer with all the sharp knives.

A record sleeve; same one that I had.

The 'Brought Back Blood' single that Nathalie had given me.

I reached into my jacket, pulled it free from the big pocket within, and held it beside this one. Just like my version, it was a black sleeve with just the scrap of paper stapled to it . . . but what was different about it was how there was a lipstick kiss smudged on over the lettering.

It was just then that I heard the key in the front door.

I looked into the drawer. Thought about the knives there. Decided against slipping one free. I glanced to the back door. Thought about running. Nah, too late now.

The front door swung open, the Spaniel stopped sniffing about my boots, and lolloped off in the direction of the new arrival, wagging its tail, respiring excitedly.

I'd never been much of a dog person.

Finally, Charles showed his face in the doorway to the kitchen.

He wore a crumpled-up suit, his tie askew. He'd probably bought the brown leather suitcase about six months before but it already had a large scuff mark.

He looked me over, and didn't look all that surprised. In fact, as he took a few steps into the kitchen, I thought I heard him breathe out a sigh. "Thought I'd be seeing you before too long," he said.

"Yeah?"

"Yeah," he replied. "You types always hang around — like the smell of dog shit."

"You gonna explain this, pal?" I said, holding up his copy of 'Brought Back Blood'.

Charles eyed the record sleeve, scowled, then shrugged. "Got it that night — the night of the show. When I asked to have it signed, all I got was some lipstick." He shrugged again. "Not really my sort of thing, anyway."

"You can say that again, mate."

Charles squared his shoulders then met me with a mean glare. "You know," he said, "you've got some nerve to break into my place and be getting shirty with me."

"Don't I know it . . ."

"What're you here for anyway?" Charles said, pulling open the cupboards, fishing out a tin of instant coffee and then setting it on the kitchen counter. He reached for the kettle, flipped it on, and the water almost immediately began to bubble away. He turned around, leaning up against the edge of the kitchen counter, eyeing me closely.

"Want to know the truth, pal."

" 'Truth' ? About what?"

"About what happened that night." I reached up, waved my hand across my face. "About what happened to that girl — Nathalie."

"Shit," Charles said, turning his gaze downwards, to the toes of his recently polished shoes. "You ain't gonna leave it be, are you?"

"Nah," I replied, still keeping the drawer full of sharp knives to the edge of my vision.

Charles sighed. "Me and Nathalie, we were an item once." He shrugged. "Thommy, he's a good boy, helps me out sometimes when I need a bit of — "

He made a gesture of puffing away on a spliff as if I might be some sort of a narc wearing a wire.

He went on. "Didn't have any ideas about going out to the Dykes show that night, not by a long shot, but when Thommy asked me for something to do, I told him that if he was looking for something authentic he should get himself down to the *Twin Turns*." He shrugged. "I ended up tagging along with him, but whatever, right?"

Realising that Charles had noted my proximity to the open knife drawer, I brought my arms up from my sides, crossed them over my chest to show him that I had no intention of making a grab for one.

"Look," Charles continued, "I ain't gonna make any trouble about you breaking and entering, or whatever. Don't want trouble, that clear? I know what it's like — know what you'll all think of me, abandoning the scene, and all, but sometimes, you know, you just want things nice for a while, if you get me?"

When I'd come to Charles's place, I'd come in hate, expecting to get myself riled by the guy. So I was somewhat surprised to find myself softening towards him . . . which was to say that I saw no reason to cause him trouble. Being a yuppie wasn't a crime after all.

"All's I want to know is who cut her up," I replied.

"Well," Charles said, "I can tell you who didn't."

"Yeah?"

"Yeah," Charles replied. "*I* didn't . . . Oh sure, me and

Nathalie we had a tough time, but nothing that'd get me into doing something like that — *nothing* like that." His expression became stern for several seconds. "That clear?"

I paused another few moments, feeling my heartbeat, steely and thick, pounding on through my veins. Finally, I nodded back at him. "Yeah," I replied, then nodded to the door. "See myself out, shall I?"

Charles shrugged. "Make you a coffee, if you like."

Shit, and just my luck to come across a nice yuppie . . .

---

That night, with the moon full and the sky clear, I trudged my way back home thinking over how I'd spent the day; and how I'd come no closer to locating the guy who'd cut Nathalie up. I suppose, in a way, it didn't really matter. And, in retrospect, I guess that Nathalie probably *knew* just who it was . . . she just didn't want to tell anybody about it. For some reason, to know that I'd been stitched up — fed to the cops — by someone else involved in the scene made it easier to stomach. It had been the idea that someone from the *outside* — some fucking *tourist* — had dobbed me in that'd rankled.

Now, if Nathalie came to me, asked to know just who did it.

Just who did *that* to her.

Then I'd listen.

And I'd do my utmost to help out.

But, somehow, I just couldn't angle my mind around that happening.

# Disappearing

4:48 a.m., 1st June 20 —

Clarence Hensman eyed the white label sewn onto his brown, canvas rucksack; the one with the well-worn leather straps. The white label bore his name: 'CLARENCE' written out in firm, black lettering — block capitals. His mother had demanded that she fasten the label on years ago, when Clarence had first decided to take the rucksack to school . . . as if he might lose it there . . . as if *some other* kid would have a rucksack which would even *approximate* the appearance of this one; mistake this rucksack for their own.

The rucksack was just about the only possession Clarence truly cherished.

His grandfather had left it to him, told him that he had used it to go trekking in the woods when he'd been younger; before his knees had become all gammy and he'd had to use a walking frame.

Clarence eyed the white label again and then did what he had fantasised about ever since the day his mother had sewn it on. He reached forward and — with an efficient twisting motion — tore the label free.

For a couple of moments, he gripped the label tightly, between finger and thumb, examining the block lettering:

CLARENCE

*CLAR*-UNCE

He had always hated his name.

Like all other kids, it'd been his parents who had chosen it for him. If he'd had his own way, he might've put in the groundwork for some kind of motion to give all kids the option to pick out their own name by the time they reached fifteen; his age now.

When they actually *understood* something about the world.

Something about themselves.

Clarence screwed the label up and tossed it into the small plastic bin in the corner of his bedroom. It unfurled itself almost as soon as it landed within since it was made of fabric; cotton, or something.

Clarence looped an arm through the shoulder strap of the rucksack, testing its weight once again. He had wanted to pack light . . . they'd all decided on that . . .

He glanced back to his bedside table, eyeing the drawer in which he had stashed his phone. It felt almost as if he was leaving a part of himself behind; as if he'd severed one of his limbs. But he'd get through.

There was a greater purpose at stake.

Hearing the twitters of the early-morning birdsong outside his window, and with the sunrise leaking in about the edges of his curtains, he picked his way through the silent house.

## 6.01 p.m., 1st June 20 —

Shirley Hensman tapped her index finger against the plastic indentation in the steering wheel. She breathed in the steady scent of exhaust fumes which snuck their way in through the air vents, and stared at the back end of the car in front.

It was one of those four-wheel drive monstrosities; the ones with the covered spare tyre hanging off the back door. Even with its engine idling, it sounded like some kind of wounded beast. Shirley strained her neck to see the other cars ahead.

She could already see the entrance to her driveway, the pair of stone-engraved pheasants which stood proud on either side of the pillars. She allowed herself a faint smile at the memory. At when her husband, Tony, had surprised her with the pair of them on their tenth wedding anniversary, telling her that they needed to 'spruce up' the place a bit.

She'd always loved his sense of humour.

A stray tear ran down her cheek.

She wiped it away with her palm.

A reflex.

The evidence dispensed with as soon as it had appeared.

She snorted air a dozen or more times.

Getting her head straight again.

She felt the car shaking. It was a fifteen-year-old estate, well-dented, and feeling as though it would fall apart at any second. Give it the open road, a nice, long stretch of motorway, smooth asphalt as far as the eye could see, and it would open up its proud, old engine . . . it seemed to struggle most at moments like these, when stuck in traffic; forced into a low gear. It might stall at any second as it had done constantly in the past — just this morning, in fact. Of course they'd often spoken about trading in and buying a newer car, but, for the time being, at least while there was still *some* life in the wreck, it didn't seem to make financial sense. They had Clarence's university days out ahead of them and every spare penny needed to be tossed into that account.

When the four-wheel drive snarled forward, Shirley flapped the accelerator, just making it into her drive before the traffic ground to a halt once again.

She stopped in the gravel driveway, losing herself in an almost hypnotic fashion in the *crunch* of the tiny rocks beneath her tyres before dragging up the handbrake, switching off the engine and resting there.

She took another few lungfuls of air.

She was certain she could still smell him.

Smell his *scent* on her.

## 6.03 p.m., 1st June 20 —

Outside, Tony Hensman heard the percussive *slam* of a car door.

It was followed by the familiar twin *chirps* of the locks snapping into place.

Tony scratched out a final line on the piece of paper, laid down his pen, and then slipped his glasses down his nose; leaving them flat across his scribblings. He reached down for the thin tyres of his wheelchair — ingrained with grit — and spun them back.

With expert control, he wheeled himself over the vinyl tiles of his office, leaving his drawing space behind; where he had been working at *Marvin and the Monkey*, a new cartoon series he had recently been commissioned for by a local zoo. The designs, as he had been told, would be used on all manner of things; chiefly on the paper placemats used in the cafeteria. He was to come up with a series of a dozen or more and, from those, the zoo would make their choices.

Once out in the hall — it also had been tiled over since his accident — he listened to the rhythmic *clack* of his wife's heels on the paving stones outside. And then the rapid *scrub* of her inserting the key into the lock. The door opened with a slight *creak* of hinges; something which he'd promised himself, weeks ago, to see to. A five-second job when he eventually got around to it.

He took in his wife; Shirley.

Today, as she had been this morning, she wore a sharp, well-cut suit.

A sable tone to it.

And a simple white blouse beneath.

Her blond hair was tucked neatly into a ponytail, and her slick, pearl-intoned skin sheened with the light in the bright, overcast early-evening sky.

A leather satchel hung off her shoulder.

She turned and closed the door behind her, shutting it with an efficient finality before turning to him, and smiling. As always, there was that momentary pause.

She swooped down and planted a kiss on his lips. "Good day?" she said, straightening up, and shifting the weight of her satchel across her lower back.

"So-so," Tony replied.

His answer was almost always the same.

Ever since he had decided to work from home, his schedule had gradually — day-after-day — moved further and further into the night.

Nowadays, he did his best work in the early hours of the morning when there were none of the daily stimulations; the cooking, cleaning . . . lubricating of hinges . . . to be done about the house.

Shirley clacked her way in through the kitchen doorway. "Clarence upstairs, doing homework?"

Tony smiled. He wheeled himself after Shirley, thinking about how that was one of those little secrets which he shared with his son . . . the fact that — by the *rules* — Clarence was meant to go directly up to his bedroom and start into the books. In theory he was meant to get done with his homework by dinner. But it didn't seem to end up that way all that often. Most likely, at this time, Clarence would be playing video games.

Some nights — in the early hours — when Tony headed for a trip to the toilet, he would hear the gentle mashing of plastic buttons from upstairs. It wasn't worth his while dragging himself upstairs to give Clarence a telling off so he would often send him a text message; something along the lines of *Big Brother is watching you.*

Soon after whichever message Tony chose to send, the tapping would stop, and silence would reign throughout the house once again; only broken by the odd scratching of Tony's pen as he worked to ink his drawings.

Tony wheeled over to the kitchen wall, to where he had left his cane leaning up in the corner. He breathed in deeply, crunched his teeth together, and then placed all his force downwards, bringing himself to his feet. Already, before he'd even put weight on his legs, he felt fatigue setting in. He reached out for his cane, knowing that Shirley was watching each and every one of his movements. He supposed, in a way, one of the other reasons he had for working late was so that Shirley wouldn't see the state he would be in after climbing the stairs; how he would have sweat oozing out of his pores all over his body.

How he'd barely be able to breathe for the exertion.

Strange to think that, before the accident, Tony had never considered himself to be anything like those touchy *macho* guys . . . the ones who'd get their knickers in a twist if anyone dared call into question their manhood.

Now, though, it seemed different.

Pride, he supposed, was all a matter of context.

Finally up on his feet, Tony seized hold of his cane, keeping himself up in a standing position. He looked over to Shirley, but she had already turned her back on him, busy cleaning a dirty coffee cup Tony had left in the kitchen sink.

He had been meaning to clean that.

Once Shirley had rinsed the cup out, she clacked her way

back across the kitchen, out into the hall and called up the stairs. "Clarence? Clarence?"

She laid a tentative foot on the first step.

Then called again.

"Clarence?"

It still sent something of a chill down Tony's spine to hear his father's name spoken out loud . . . used to refer to another human being . . . his own son . . . but it had been Shirley's choice; she was a keen follower of family tradition and simply *liked* the name.

When Tony heard no reply to Shirley's calls, he limped his way out into the hall; favouring his better left leg as he went.

Standing beside her, he called up.

Called his father's name.

"Clarence!" he said, a touch of anger in his tone.

9:11 p.m., 1st June 20 —

It was beautiful to watch the sun going down — more beautiful than Clarence ever would've imagined. He peered out through the pine trees. He took in the chocolatey soil which spanned the space between. And then he tuned into the merry birdsong.

Funny to think that paradise had only ever been a few hours' bus ride away.

He reached up and ran his thumb about the collar of the black shirt he had put on that morning. It was something of a tick he had developed at school. Whenever he'd felt the glare of a teacher passing over the rows, looking for someone to pick on for an answer. Realising this, he pulled his hands away from his collar. There was *none* of that stuff now — that stuff was all in the past. He had escaped . . . *disappeared.*

From his side, he heard a spluttering cough.

He turned to look.

Alexandra and Peterson sat beside him, on the grass; their own rucksacks laid down in their laps. They were passing a spliff between the two of them. Catching Clarence's eye, Alexandra offered it to him, but Clarence shook his head and smiled.

"Best way to enjoy a sunset," Alexandra said . . . she would near enough chop off anybody's head who dared to call her 'Alex'.

"It's fine," Clarence replied, turning back to the fiery glow as it dipped below the horizon; ruffled by the ragged outlines of the pine trees.

There was a long pause while the sun finally disappeared,

and then, with a spluttering cough, Alexandra said, "So, how does it feel to be a criminal?"

"A 'criminal' ?" Clarence replied, looking back at her.

Alexandra had honey-blond hair and long eyelashes. She also had a whole scattering of freckles which, until today, he hadn't noticed. He wondered if she had used some sort of concealer to keep *that* particular aspect secret at school.

Girls could be mean, from what Clarence had heard.

"Uh-huh," Alexandra said, jabbing the finished-with spliff into the soil. She peered back at him from beneath lowered lids. "It's against the *law* to skip school."

Clarence wasn't certain what he felt about that. He shot Peterson a quick glance, wondering if this was some sort of joke he hadn't quite cottoned onto.

Peterson had slick, black hair and dark, handsome features. Like Alexandra, he wore a hooded sweatshirt, though he kept the hood drawn up at all times; a baseball cap was also locked onto his scalp.

All throughout the journey so far, Clarence had wondered just what sort of image Peterson had been trying to cultivate. If he was trying to act as some sort of a *hard case* among them, to steer off any danger.

Truth be told, though, there wasn't really any danger to be had.

"Do kids go to prison for it?" Clarence said.

"Prison for what?" Alexandra replied.

"For skipping school?"

Alexandra rolled her eyes; one of those infantile gestures which she seemed to find so attractive . . . "Doubt it," she replied, and then glanced to Peterson, smiling at him; the two of them sharing some private joke.

Clarence turned his attention back to the landscape.

He thought on how this had all come about.

It had been a message to his personal email; not to his *school* account, of course. And the message had been signed as coming from Alexandra and Peterson. He had no idea why they'd picked him — he wasn't *friends* with them, or anything — and when, on the bus up here, he'd put the question to the two of them, Peterson had just sort of smirked and said that he'd thought his name was 'goofy'.

Well, Clarence's name might've been 'goofy' but at least he went by his first name, rather than his surname, as if he was some sort of prima donna.

When Clarence had asked the two of them if they'd wanted anyone else to come along, they'd got evasive, but, from their answers he could tell that they'd certainly sounded others out. As they had drawn closer to their destination, and with Alexandra apparently growing more trusting in his company, she had revealed that he was the only one who they'd actually approached directly about this running-away thing.

That had only led to more questions.

Again, *why him* . . . he wasn't going to buy that Peterson had simply thought his name was 'goofy'.

Finally, Alexandra had relented and said that Clarence had seemed so 'in his own head' about school, and that he was a stone clad picture of a runaway.

What one of those might look like, Clarence really hadn't the faintest idea.

As he stared into the darkness, watching the first of the bats meandering about the evening thermals, catching bugs, chittering to one another, he wondered if he would've accepted Alexandra and Peterson's offer if he'd been clear they were a couple — or, at the very least, an *emerging* couple . . . there were few worse things than being a spare wheel . . .

He turned to them now, Peterson and Alexandra close, but not touching.

Their heads inclined, one into the other.

And their fingers, splayed to support their weight on the ground, nearly in contact.

"Do you think they'll find us?" Clarence asked.

Peterson turned to him first.

But he didn't respond.

When Alexandra turned to him, she had that same slightly bitter expression sketched all across her face. "That's not the point," she said. "That's not the *joke.*"

"Oh," Clarence replied, meeting her eyes and feeling like some sort of scolded puppy. He hated the way that Alexandra and Peterson made him feel, as if he was just some stupid, naïve little kid . . . come to think of it, how his *parents* had made him feel . . . what had made him *want* to run away in the first place . . .

Alexandra leaned away from Peterson.

She brought her palm up before her and jabbed a single finger down on her skin. "We hide out here a week or so" — she jabbed a pair of fingers into her palm — "then we return. Show up back home." She jabbed three fingers down on her palm now. "No explanations. No apologies. We pretend that nothing happened at all."

And even though she was explaining it exactly as she had on the bus trip up here, Clarence still didn't quite understand.

Why would he want to return home at all?

## 11:44 a.m., 2nd June 20 —

Shirley was sure that she'd felt the heel going even as she'd stepped out of the car.

But she'd paid it no mind.

She had been in a rush . . . no time to waste.

It was when she'd turned the corner, put a little extra weight on her right foot, that she'd felt her ankle slipping away from her; almost as if she might've been attempting to run on ice. She'd attempted to arrest her fall but been unable to do so.

And then she'd tumbled down.

Hit *hard* against the well-polished, tiled floor of her office corridor.

She'd thought quickly enough to reach out and break her fall.

And she'd felt the sharp pain in her left elbow as she'd struck.

Thankfully, there'd been no one to see her fall . . . no one to fawn over her misfortune.

In silence, teeth sunk into her lip, tasting blood, she'd brought herself back up to her feet and limped her way onward.

When she'd reached the office itself, she'd had the good sense to slip off both of her shoes so that she wouldn't resemble some sort of half-mauled antelope. In fact, she managed to reach her cubicle without anybody commenting on anything else other than to wish her a Good Morning.

It was only when she sat down in her chair, felt the articulated parts taking her weight, and she stared at her email inbox tray that she realised just how futile it had been to drag herself into work today.

Her son, Clarence, had gone missing.

There had been no note.

No signs of forced kidnapping.

And nothing to be done.

Shirley and her husband Tony had been up all night, speaking with Clarence's school — with the police. They'd driven around the neighbourhood, and then the town searching. Shirley had tried calling his phone over and over again, before she'd heard it vibrating to itself in the drawer of Clarence's bedside table. With his phone in hand, she had set about calling through the entire list of contacts — all of them kids Clarence's own age, his schoolmates — but not one of them had had any idea where Clarence might be.

In the end, it must've been around three or four o'clock in the morning when she'd sent a message to her boss telling him that she would be in later that day; that she needed to get some sleep after the fraught night she'd had. Her boss, of course, trying her best to be understanding, had told her that there was no need for her to come into work that day . . . but Shirley had insisted.

It was only when she caught motion out of the corner of her eye that she realised that he had arrived; that *Mark* had returned to the office from wherever he'd been . . . perhaps meeting with a client.

As always, he was wearing a sweeping gabardine coat.

As elegant as ever.

She took in his greyed hair and his still-youthful, smooth skin . . . the skin which she had felt alongside her own more times than she wished to think about during a stolen afternoon or an early-morning 'visit to the gym'.

It would've been naïve to think that her and Mark's affair had escaped the attention of the office, and it would've been all the more naïve to think that there was anything but the faintest shred of interest surrounding their fling.

They weren't the first.

And they most certainly wouldn't be the last.

Sometimes it made Shirley smile through the tears to think that some people thought working in accounts might be dull, when it was anything but.

If she ordinarily put up at least the vaguest of fronts to her office colleagues, then today it completely fell away. She stood up from her cubicle, her high heels discarded beneath her desk, and she padded across the carpet to Mark in only her tights.

Mark greeted her with the same smile as always, although she noted the slight expression of concern. He could surely tell that she wasn't her normal self.

Although, more than anything else, Shirley had wanted to call Mark up last night, to tell him what was going on, they had made it a rule never to speak of things between them any other way except face-to-face.

Mark, too, had a family he wished to preserve beyond this affair.

His touch was sure, and firm, as he rested his hand on her forearm, guiding her into one of the deserted offices to the side of the main area. Once inside, he shut the door and brought the blinds down so that they'd have some privacy.

Out of the window, Shirley could see the golden late-morning sunlight beaming down on the fluttering leaves of the elm trees.

This should've been a normal day.

A day like *any* other.

Sobbing more than once, Shirley beat through the night's events, relaying them as they occurred to her. When she was finally finished, she looked to Mark, feeling a pair of tears roll down her cheeks. She knew that she must look a real mess.

"Okay," Mark said, apparently taking it all in. "I think there's someone I can call."

Shirley was surprised at the thump her heart gave.

At how it felt almost as if a weight had been lifted off her shoulders.

"*Really*?" she said.

Mark reached into the inside pocket of his coat and withdrew his phone. Without another word, he flicked through his contact list. He glanced up, smiled briefly, then said, "Go home. Get some rest. I'll get in touch when I know something, all right?"

Shirley was so pleased to hear this, to know that *something* was being done about Clarence's disappearance, that she simply nodded, and left the room.

It was only when she got to the car park that she realised she still wore only her tights; and that she'd left her defective high heels up in the office.

Underneath her desk.

## 1:52 a.m., 3rd June 20 —

Tony had tried to do some drawing, if only as a kind of coping mechanism. But stress had a habit of seizing hold of him and grinding him down into the ground. Whenever he picked up his pen to ink this or that, an uncontrollable shaking prevented him so much as marking a dot on the page.

His son was still gone.

Upstairs, he could hear his wife Shirley coughing; constantly turning over in bed.

He knew that she was waiting for him to go up.

She needed some company.

Someone to share her *fear* with.

And yet, Tony found it difficult to do that.

Even before the accident, he hadn't been the most affectionate of husbands. He had had his spaces, his interests, while Shirley had had her own.

The accident had only demarcated those boundaries further.

Sometimes he wondered if it might be about the sex — about the fact that, no matter what the doctors said, that Tony was one-hundred-per-cent recovered Down There — he could never manage to get himself 'in the mood'.

Did that hurt their intimacy?

Did it somehow make them less of a couple?

. . . And, worse, had Clarence somehow sensed that yawning, growing distance?

They always said that children were perceptive, didn't they?

Did Clarence even qualify as a child any longer?

Tony really hadn't a clue . . .

He just seemed so distant from everyone now.
From *everything*.
From himself.

5:52 a.m., 3rd June 20 —

Clarence couldn't help but wake with the sunlight as it crested the valley, as it splashed playfully against the orange canvas of his tent, setting his surroundings in a kind of ethereal glow. When he reached out and tugged the zip to the tent flap open, he was surprised at the cool breeze which blew. It almost had a bite of ice to it; bringing the blood rising to the surface of his cheeks.

He looked about the camp, to the equipment they had brought.

The brand-new gas stove.

And the cooling boxes stashed full of food.

Alexandra and Peterson had thought of everything; or so it seemed.

Clarence remembered standing at the till in the camping supplies shop and being taken aback at the total cost of the purchases. He had never imagined that living an outdoors life would be such an *expensive* ordeal. He'd been surprised again when they'd gone by the supermarket to stock up on supplies for the week . . . to tell the truth, he'd never paid much attention to his parents' shopping habits; to the cost of every last thing in their cupboards, fridge and freezer.

When Clarence had offered to pay, even though he had no money on him, Alexandra and Peterson had simply smirked. Told him that he was their 'guest' for the week.

. . . Just what they exactly meant by that had passed Clarence by.

He crawled into the porch section of his tent and jabbed his feet into a pair of well-battered trainers he'd kicked off the night before. To think that he'd used these same trainers for PE only a day or so ago . . . that seemed a world away now.

Almost like a past life.

12:10 p.m., 3rd June 20 —

Shirley jumped when her mobile buzzed to signal a call.

Sunlight beamed in around the perimeter of the curtains.

Midday.

And it felt hot . . . *humid* out.

She snatched up the handset lying on her bedside table, and then, seeing the name displayed on the screen — *Mark* — glanced to the doorway.

Just as her office probably knew of their affair, she couldn't quite believe that Tony didn't suspect *something* . . . their relationship had shifted so much since his accident; almost so that it hardly represented whatever it had been before.

She answered the call and held the handset to her ear.

She heard Mark's breathing before she heard his words.

"Shirl?" Mark said.

"Yes?"

"I think I've got some useful information — something to pass onto the police."

Shirley sat up in bed.

"It's some information on purchases; some purchases reported on a stolen credit card."

Shirley felt the breath leave her lungs.

All of a sudden she was weak.

A tingling sensation passed over the surface of her skin.

"Go on," she said, her voice raspy, uneven; ready to crack at any moment.

"Camping supplies," he said.

" 'Camping' ?"

"That's right."

Shirley stayed very still, staring at the white-washed wall of their bedroom. Just now she noticed that there was a scuffmark about halfway up. She supposed it was some relic from when she'd dressed herself in the dark, as she always did, never wanting to wake Tony . . . never daring to so much as touch him in his sleep lest he'd wake up and she'd be forced into kissing him goodbye. Those morning kisses, knowing she was going to the office — going to be with Mark — seemed almost like tiny betrayals to her.

. . . Oh, *God* . . . what had she got herself into?

Mark remained on the line.

His breathing heavy.

She pictured him at the office; peering out the window, down onto the courtyard garden, one finger pressed to his temple as he often stood whenever speaking on the phone with a client. That was how she felt now.

Like a *client.*

"Shirl?" Mark said.

"Yes?"

A long pause, and then, "Nothing. I just hope that this ends up okay, that's all."

Strangely, Shirley felt a smile sneak onto her lips, though she gathered no joy from it. It felt as if all the joy had been sucked out from her leaving nothing but a void in her chest.

"See you soon," she said.

Another pause, then, "Yeah, Shirl, see you soon."

Mark hung up.

For several minutes, Shirley remained in the same posture, her phone pressed to the side of her head, staring into mid-air.

During that time, she thought of nothing at all.
Did she even *feel* anything anymore?

5:36 p.m., 3rd June 20 —

Tony glanced up to the window of his home office.

As always, he had shut the blind to stop the sun coming in and making the room unbearably hot. It was easy for this room to get like that in summer.

Outside, he could hear the *rumble* of a car engine.

A car turning into the driveway.

He set down his pen on his desk; peeled his glasses off the ridge of his nose.

Although he hadn't realised it as he'd been drawing, he was sweating all over.

When a cool draught blowing through the house caught his dampened skin, he felt a shudder pass over him with a skittish sensation. He reached down, disengaged the brake on his wheelchair, and spun himself backwards.

As he wheeled himself into the front hall, he heard the gentle *thud* of his wife Shirley's footsteps on the staircase. She was out of bed, obviously having anticipated the visitor. Someone she had been expecting. But since Tony hadn't been able to concentrate on his work, and considering that he was here — *at the door* — now, it seemed a silly thing to leave it to her. He opened the door to reveal a pair of men.

One of them was dressed in a simple, cheap-looking suit; the kind that supermarkets would sell as 'washing-machine ready'. The other, a few sheepish paces back, wore a gabardine coat. He held his hands down at his side in such a way that suggested, to Tony, he really wanted nothing more but to stick them in his pockets; and perhaps to bow his head.

To *disappear.*

Tony took in the first man again.

Blond, balding hair.

Bright-blue eyes.

A doughy, almost childlike jaw.

Tony's brain, as it always did, worked to subconsciously file away those details for later use in one of his panels. It would come out sooner or later — a face from the past — and he would experience that rather *eerie* moment as he attempted to place the sudden recognition.

"Mr Hensman?"

"Yes?"

The blond-haired man in the cheap suit glanced to the man behind him.

Then back to Tony.

"I'm a private investigator," he said. "There's something you'll want to see. About your son."

"About my son?" Tony echoed, sounding, even to himself, as if he had slipped away into some daze.

Only when Tony glanced back to the staircase did he realise that Shirley had come down from the bedroom, and that she crouched in the middle of the steps; her arms childishly wrapped about her kneecaps, drawing them into her chest.

Tony finally regained his senses.

He pressed on a smile.

"Please," he said, to the two men. "Please do come in."

## 3:55 p.m., 4th June 20 —

Clarence was only certain he heard voices when he turned his head in their direction; when he felt his ears prick up; *analyse* the sound.

Yes, there were certainly people here.

He glanced over their camp, and then looked into the distance, in the direction of the stream, where Alexandra and Peterson had disappeared about ten minutes before.

He knew that they should've pitched camp somewhere else; somewhere further away from the main path. But, on that first day — the day they'd arrived here — Clarence hadn't felt it his place to comment on any of Alexandra and Peterson's decisions.

He hadn't yet felt a member of the group.

. . . He *still* didn't feel a member of the group.

Just as he had feared, Alexandra and Peterson had been carrying out their flirtations in front of him, dragging him on as some sort of a witness; for whatever demented reason they might require one.

Clarence glanced down to his rucksack.

It lay just outside his tent, leaning up against the canvas.

He thought about it for a second.

Another.

And then he grabbed it and ran.

## 3:56 p.m., 4th June 20 —

Shirley felt her skin itching. She knew that the mosquitos were biting, and that they'd only get worse as the evening drew on. She hadn't had time to pick out a proper outfit for this expedition, and had ended up settling on a blue-grey tracksuit now a couple of sizes too large. She supposed it'd been one of those forgotten pregnancy purchases; one of those snap decisions she had made in the name of comfort. If she hadn't found it bundled up at the bottom of her wardrobe, she might never have believed that it belonged to her at all.

George, the private investigator, trod on ahead.

Mark trailed just behind.

Shirley had seen the looks which'd passed between the two of them, no matter how *subtle* they had tried to be about it. She knew the two of them viewed her as some sort of ticking time bomb, primed to explode at any given second.

They had left Tony back in the car, of course, despite his protests; his wheelchair still folded up in the backseat and his cane all but useless in the boot.

The attendant back at the car park had informed them about the children he'd seen, the ones with the camping gear. The details had squared with the research George had done . . . the stolen credit card report he had found on some Godforsaken police database. The reason George, and Mark, had come over to the house was because it was on George's advice that they *not* pass this particular information over to the police.

Running away was one thing.

Credit-card fraud quite another.

. . . And even though they were still minors, it was something which none of the children would enjoy having on their record later on in life.

They needed to catch the kids before they did themselves any more damage.

It was then that Shirley heard voices up ahead. The gentle *scrunch-scrunch* of footsteps against dirt.

George surprised her by breaking into a run.

He cleared the trees ahead, crested the hill, and disappeared from sight.

Shirley glanced back to Mark, and then the two hurried on after him.

4:19 p.m., 4th June 20 —

Tony sat in the baking-hot car.

*Their* car . . . Shirley's car.

Trees sprung up all around him.

*Pines.*

On the armrest of the passenger seat, he jabbed the button for the automatic window, but, of course, there being no power to the engine, it didn't shift at all.

At least the private investigator — and *That Man* — had had the awareness to leave the window open a few fingers, otherwise Tony might well have suffocated by now.

Like some baby, or a *dog* . . .

Something caught the corner of his eye.

He turned in his seat.

Analysed the figure striding across the car park.

At first, he didn't recognise his own son.

It was only when he took in the rucksack — his *father's* rucksack — slung over the boy's shoulder that he realised who it was.

All at once, Tony found himself filled with joy, and exasperation.

He swivelled about in his chair, shouting at the top of his lungs.

"Hey! Hey! *HEY*!"

Clarence stopped, pivoted, and looked absent-mindedly in Tony's direction. For a moment, their gaze seemed to cross, and then Clarence sprinted away.

Tony called out again. "HEY!"

But Clarence had cleared the car park.

Thinking quickly, Tony scrabbled about, unlatched the door, and then — leaning against the car; sweating all over — made for the boot where they'd put his cane.

## 4:22 p.m., 4th June 20 —

As Clarence drew in the gushing sound of the river — in the unseen ravine below — his feet slipped several times on the dirt path. He gripped on tight to his rucksack, drew it closer to his shoulder, determined not to let it go. He skipped over the roots which jutted up out of the earth. And felt the scratch of the pine needles as he passed them by.

He was still in shock after seeing his father.

The question of *how* rattled through his mind again and again and again, and he continued to wrestle to uncover some feasible answer.

In the end, he was forced to turn his concentration to the matter at hand.

To his escape.

He knew that there were others with his father — it was their voices which had first alerted him to their presence. Others more able-bodied. And he knew that they wouldn't face the same obstacles his father would in pursuing him.

Clarence moved quickly, getting himself down to the river bank. He felt his foot sink into the soft, silty soil at the side of the gushing water. The air seemed to be at its hottest at this time, though he could already feel the sun's strength waning. He looked to the stepping stones which led across the river and knew that this was his means of escape . . . they might never catch him if he made his way across to the other side.

He would have disappeared forever.

4:31 p.m., 4th June 20 —

Shirley took up the lead as Mark and George frogmarched the boy and girl along the forest path, and back towards the car park.

She had had to step in and stop George from going into good-cop/bad-cop mode; raising the issue that the recovery of her *son* was the be-all and end-all of this impromptu expedition. And that, in the wider scheme of things, she couldn't care less about the other two kids except perhaps later as some kind of means to cleanse her own son's name of this credit-card fraud business.

When they reached the car park, Shirley was surprised to see that the car door was open, and that Tony was no longer sat within. She saw that the boot, too, had been popped.

Already, she had an inkling of what had happened.

And there was simply no time for her to explain.

Mark and George understood on some intuitive level and they hurried on after her with their captives.

Shirley felt the tears streaking her cheeks as she dashed down the hillside, employing amateur tracker skills in following the lagging gait of her husband; the lazy sweep of the afflicted right leg which he dragged behind him when employing a cane.

Finally, she got herself down to the river bank.

Found herself staring at her husband's turned back as he, in turn, stared at the stepping stones positioned in the stream; leaning on his cane for balance.

"Where is he?" Shirley said, through stifled breaths. "Where's Clarence?"

Slowly, Tony turned to her.
A doleful expression on his face.

4:33 p.m., 4th June 20 —

Tony stared back at his wife; to her tangled-up, misplaced blond hair. He took in, too, the sweat patches at each of her armpits, and at her chest; between her breasts.

She always had everything so together.

He had always felt so *inferior* to her when it came to being organised . . . when it came to giving nothing away to the wider world. He had always been the emotional one while she had been calm, collected, *laid-back*.

Now, though, he could tell that the roles were reversed.

His heart thumped on gently.

Almost placidly.

"Where's Clarence?" Shirley repeated.

Tony followed her eyes for a few more seconds and then turned back to the river before him. He looked off downstream.

Apparently realising that a sense of urgency wasn't going to draw the information out of him, Shirley sidled up beside him. He could tell she was putting great effort into keeping her voice even. But he could still sense the frayed nature of her tone.

Eighteen years of marriage didn't teach you anything if it didn't teach you how to second guess your partner's every waking thought and desire.

"Did he cross the river?" Shirley said.

Tony shook his head. "No. He didn't."

"How'd you know? You couldn't have kept up with him. Not with your cane."

Tony winced a little at her icy tone, but he otherwise didn't respond.

He thought about the last time they had had a fight — a *proper* fight.

It was probably ten years ago now . . . that was how long it had taken him to realise that he could never possibly win against her.

"No footprints," Tony said, making a point of raising his cane to indicate the opposing bank of the river. "These stones are all partially submerged. If Clarence had gone across then he would've left a trail." He turned to Shirley now. "Don't you think?"

Shirley nodded back, apparently numbed by this knowledge. And then, as if something had stirred within her, she turned her head back to the water; moving her attention downstream. "You think . . ." she said, but trailed off.

"I *think*," Tony went on, his breathing still feeling a touch shallow from the exertion, "that he'll come back home when he's good and ready."

Shirley's eyes widened in alarm. "But what if he's . . ."

Tony cut through her without needing to raise his voice.

It was enough to simply keep a cool head.

"He's a good swimmer," Tony said. "And if we keep on chasing him then he'll keep on running . . . even if we catch him, bring him back home."

Shirley stared, dead-eyed, at the water as it swilled about the rocks.

She parted her lips to say something, but she made no sound in the end.

And Tony knew that he'd won this particular 'argument'.

"Come on," Tony said, lifting up an arm and placing it carefully on his wife's shoulder, "let's go and see how those other kids are doing — I bet they're scared stiff . . . probably think that we're the police or something."

He gave Shirley's shoulder a tight squeeze and then shifted his attention to the hillside ahead. It would be a long, hard slog to the top with just his cane.

But he would manage.

It must've taken Tony the best part of half an hour to reach the top of the valley which encased the river, and when he did, he glanced back; saw that Shirley continued to stand on the bank, staring into the water.

Whatever it was that she was hoping to see — whatever it was she was hoping to *find* — Tony really couldn't have said.

If she was looking for Clarence then she was better off searching elsewhere.

Because Clarence was gone.

He had disappeared.

# Shadow Struck

## I

It was something about the way the shadows moved, outside the window. The way that they played across the grassy bank — almost like rising, sable flames, before simmering down to mere embers. It always happened this way, at this time of day; around sunset.

On the banks of the River Cam.

At first Lola had thought about changing her lodgings: the canal boat moored to the bank of Jesus Green. She had believed, when she decided to base herself here, on the water, that the nausea of the constantly moving canal boat would soon enough drive her away.

However, that hadn't been an issue at all.

*That* wasn't what threatened to drive her away.

The issue which *had* come to bother her was the shadows.

In fact, they had grown to bother her to such a degree that she had *actually* thought about upping sticks, forgoing the deposit she had put down — six months' rent in advance — and finding someplace else.

Somewhere far away from the water.

Although she never would've admitted as much out loud — she had enough trouble admitting it to herself — she woke from feverish dreams, in the middle of the day; in the darkness, her duvet all scrunched up at the foot of her bed: breathing hard, sodden with sweat; thinking about those shadows.

She breathed in deeply, and lightly pressed her forehead to the glass. She stared out across the mulchy, grey-brown river water. The glass was cool against her skin, and the smell of the glass, and the dust clinging to it, put her in mind of blood.

She could still taste the blood at the back of her mouth, from last night's feed.

From the unsuspecting student she had briefly grappled with, before clutching the chloroform-doused rags over his lips.

He had been wearing his Cambridge University graduation robes — the same shade of black as the shadows outside her window — and as Lola had lowered him gently down onto the cobbled streets, she had smelled the heady scent of whisky clinging to him. She had presumed that he had stopped by his tutor's quarters, that he had attended some private celebration before returning to the *real* party. But he had never arrived.

As she had read in the news, the police had found his body earlier in the day, floating along in the river. Another drunken drowning. Little would be made of the fang marks in his neck. The half pint of purloined blood.

No, those would be mere *details* in so straight-forward a case.

She had seen it before *so many* times.

How humans — how what she had *once* been — refused to see the truth for themselves; to see what was really there lurking just below the surface.

Lola stared out through the glass.

What *was* causing the odd effect of the shadows?

Was it some overheated rooftop, giving off waves of warmth?

Was it the way the willow trees lazily dangled their leaves in the river, and how they dappled the light?

She was unsure of the science behind it — there was only so much that *science* could explain — all she wished for was some explanation.

Something which would clue her into *an* explanation.

Was that so much to ask?

Over her shoulder, she heard the *tick-tick-tick* of the rotating pendulum of the carriage clock which sat on the mantelpiece. It, too, with the rest of the antiquated furnishings — the unpolished oak chair-and-table set; the obscure, dusty oil paintings with the gilt and silver frames — had come with the canal boat. She turned to examine the face of the carriage clock, saw that she had another fifteen minutes until she would be safe — safe to go outside.

*Oh, the price of immortality.*

At this time, she was at her most restless. Unable to stand still. Unable to *sit.* Only bundling back and forth, awaiting her opportunity. Wanting to seize the chance when it came. If she wanted to — if she *really* wanted to — she could cross the threshold, haul herself up onto the grassy bank, burn herself into cinders out in the sunlight. Be finished with this bagatelle of a half-life she had carved out for herself . . . or would it be like always; would she have to move on to some other location? When — despite keeping all those who attempted to invade her life at an arm's length — one of them managed to get in?

Because one *always* managed to get in.

She returned to the window, peered out through the glass, to those shadows as they continued to flicker against the grassy bank. And then she heard a knock at the door.

Was there anything more unnerving than unexpected visitors?

She thought long and hard about not answering, about simply staying by the window, and peering out across the water at the shadows as they played for the final — *dying* — moments of the day.

But then the knock came again.

Something like a shiver passed over the surface of her skin. A sense of urgency gripped her. She padded — *bare-footed* — across the exposed, weathered floorboards of the barge, and to the front door. She thought briefly about answering the door in her present state — wearing the floating, virginally white nightie she had slept in during the day — and she decided that nothing was to be done . . .

In any case, she liked the way the white material set off her dark-red hair, drawing a sort of *shocking* attention to it.

She jabbed her thumb down on the latch, drew the door open and peered out.

A policeman.

He looked to be in his late twenties, perhaps his early thirties. He had wispy, silver-blond hair and wore his black, sleeveless policeman's jacket over the top of a pristine white shirt. He had a tie knotted on, too, in that rather *quaint* way. His flat cap, with the black-and-white chequered pattern about its brim hypnotised her for a moment. "Evening, madam," he said, giving her a firm nod. He stood with his feet a shoulders-width apart, as if he didn't quite trust the boat's ballast.

She felt herself somewhat stunned for a couple of seconds, and then she blinked away her daze. She looked out, beyond him, to the last of the sunlight dribbling away.

To those streaky shadows on the grassy banks beyond.

If she wished — if she *really* wanted — she could easily dash out there, knock the policeman from her path, and feel herself burn out of existence in the dying light.

Right before his eyes.

"A few questions, if you wouldn't mind?" he said, and then reached up and knocked the visor of his cap back a fraction. "It's about the drowning last night — I'm sure you've read about it."

She turned her attention to the policeman's eyes — to his

clear *blue* eyes — and she realised he was awaiting her response. "Oh, yes," she replied, putting on a smile. "I . . . I'm sorry . . ."

"I've woken you," the policeman said, his smile creasing the corners of his eyes. "Sorry about that. Getting late, I know." Here his cheeks coloured slightly with a blush.

She *knew* she perhaps should've thrown a coat about her shoulders — to at least give herself *some* semblance of modesty. But, then again, she had never felt all that bad about making men feel a little uneasy. That was one of the more subtle womanly tricks — one of the masterstrokes which her kind possessed. Deciding to press her advantage, she reached out and rested her arm up against the doorframe, accentuating her presence. "Yes, I heard about it."

The policeman padded his jacket vest, then dipped his fingers into one of the pockets. From within, he removed a notepad — *paper*; again somewhat quaint. He produced a stub of pencil then flipped the page a couple of times to reach a fresh sheet. As he spoke, he leaned back slightly on his heels, tilted his head to one side, and widened his eyes in a way — Lola supposed — which was meant to paint him as being unselfconscious. "The body was found at five a.m. this morning, caught in the canal" — he jerked his thumb casually over his shoulder to indicate the direction — "dog walker," he said, with a smile, glancing up at her, "Always seems that way, doesn't it?"

"What does?"

The policeman coloured a little more at the cheeks. "I mean, a dog walker always seems to be the one to turn up the body."

"Uh-huh," she said, looking beyond the policeman, seeing the last of the shadows fade into the oncoming night.

The policeman scratched the back of his neck and then

turned to his notepad. "Well, did you see anything that you might consider to be suspicious?"

Lola felt a slight tingle down her spine to hear the word 'suspicious' being thrown around. "No, nothing that I can recall."

"Okey doke," the policeman said, and then took a step back from the doorway.

Before he completely turned around, to head off on his merry way, he glanced back over his shoulder — to Lola. "Just one more thing," he said.

"Yes?"

The policeman blushed even more — if at all possible. "You wouldn't be interested in going out for a drink with me later, would you?"

She felt her blood cool.

A strange sense of calm descended over her.

## II

The policeman picked a new pub for them to meet up later on in the evening — at least, it was a place Lola had never seen before; The Rusted Mill.

She wandered through the beer garden at around nine o'clock that night, drinkers occupying the picnic benches outside, chatting merrily; several of them chuckling away.

Not having arranged exactly *where* she would meet with the policeman — who hadn't yet thought to tell her his name.

She emerged through a pair of glass doors and out onto a wooden jetty at the back of the pub. As she glanced across the four or five tables there, she caught sight of the policeman — now dressed in a black shirt and a pair of stone-washed blue jeans.

He rose up out of his seat when he saw her, grinning from ear to ear, and blushing thickly once again. "Hi," he said, in a bright voice.

"Hi," she replied, sinking down into the seat opposite.

She shrugged off her beige cashmere coat — *far* too warm for the evening — and hung it up off the back of her chair. She was well aware of showing off the simple, black cocktail dress which she wore underneath. And which she had ensured would reach only just above the knee. She wanted to have the policeman's undivided attention, after all.

In the distance, she made out a pair of punts — like flat-bottomed Venetian gondolas — filled with giggling women and chortling men; the punters standing on the back end, sinking the wooden pole into the silt bed of the Cam, propelling them silently into the night. Some of them had thought to arrange tea lights around the periphery of the punt, and the flames of the candles flickered in the almost non-existent breeze.

Sitting at the back of the pub, she could smell the thick scent of beer mixed up with the stale odour of the river itself: rat piss mingled with who-knew-what-else.

Blood?

The policeman finally got around to introducing himself and it turned out his name was Benjamin — *not* Ben, and *not* Benny.

He had taken the trouble of ordering a drink for her already; a gin and tonic, while he had gone for a pint of ale. From the looks of his complexion, this wasn't his *first* one either.

He spoke evenly, almost too quietly to hear every word. Each time he spoke, he would lean over the table so that she could hear him. Each time, she would catch a whiff of his cologne. It smelled something between lime and jasmine, and she found herself wondering who might've picked it out for him.

His mother?

An ex-girlfriend?

An ex-*wife*?

. . . Or perhaps a *current* wife . . .

As the conversation went on, she decided that the former guess was the most likely. He told her all about how his passion — his *real* passion — was not for police work but for collectable toy cars. And only once he had gone through the entire decade of the sixties, did she realise that — free drink, or not — she wasn't going to be polite any longer.

Staring across the table at him, and hearing the chatter of the other pub goers over her shoulder, she broke through his diatribe. "About that body you turned up, are you treating it as suspicious?"

He leaned back from the table, taking his elbows off the

surface. His smile slipped a little. He studied her for a long while, then cocked his head to one side. The smile returned, but not with its former brilliance — the brilliance which'd accompanied the enthusiasm for his collectable toy cars. "I can't really say anything — it's an ongoing . . ."

Lola picked her moment and — very subtly — and without batting so much as an eyelash, she slipped her foot free of the flat shoes she wore and rubbed her bare foot up the inside of his leg. She could tell, from his reaction that he wasn't exactly accustomed to this sort of female attention — at least not to the degree that he could 'play it cool.'

His eyes bulged in their sockets. He glanced about in a panic, as if his superior — whoever that might be — could be lurking nearby, ready to pull him up for the slightest of infractions.

Lola vaguely wondered if what he was doing — taking a possible witness out for a drink — was strictly above board with the local constabulary. She couldn't care less, of course. She just wanted information. And she could *get at it* through him.

Once more, just as he had when he'd spoken at length about his collectable toy cars, Benjamin leaned in over the table conspiratorially. "The body," he said, blinking rapidly, but apparently regaining some of his initial composure. "Right, yes, well" — he glanced about again, then looked long and hard at the river before turning back to Lola — "*actually*, now that you mention it, we *are* working on the assumption that the suicides might be, uh" — Lola gave him a little more encouragement, running her foot a little further up his thigh. He blinked another few times to get his wind back — "*connected*," he got out, finally.

" 'Connected' ?" she replied, bringing her foot down from his inner leg, and instead reaching up to curl a strand of her hair about her little finger. "How?"

"Well, uh," Benjamin continued, his gaze again avoiding hers, and his fingers rubbing the condensation on the outside of his beer glass. "We turned up another body — a few weeks ago — I'm sure you read about that one, too. In a field. Strangulation. Then there was the one from a month or so ago, found him with his wrists slashed beside a dual carriageway . . ."

She cocked her head to one side in what she believed to be a *ditsy* sort of way. "Hmm?"

"Yes," Benjamin said, and then tapped at his neck, "both of them with bite marks, just like with this victim — the one we pulled out of the river this morning."

" 'Bite marks' ?" Lola repeated, and then, deciding to push her luck, "Like a *vampire?*"

Benjamin blinked several times, then said, "Yes, if you like." He then got a little irritable. He wiped long and hard at his beer glass before glancing back up and saying, "Listen, all right, the public's not privy to any of this information — as far as *they* know they've all been suicides . . . and that's the story we're sticking with until we get any further information."

"And what sort of information would that be?"

His smile had completely vanished now. He stared hard into the amber trickle of ale remaining in the base of his glass, then said — to his glass, "Need something more solid — better evidence . . . somebody who might've *seen* the bugger."

There was a long silence after his reply before she followed up by reaching for her gin and tonic for the first time, bringing it to her lips, and then drinking long and *thirstily*.

When she set the drink down on the table between them with a glassy *thunk*, she caught his eyes with her own. "I want you to take me home."

## III

On the walk back from the pub, Lola found herself reeling through the options open to her at this point. From the information she had garnered this evening from Benjamin, she had established that the police were onto her — that, if she wished to survive then she desperately needed to flee town, and move over to another.

She wondered if she might head down south — *back to London* — it was simple to lose herself there, in such an urban sprawl; so many bizarre occurrences, so many *suicides*.

Yes, she would have little trouble concealing herself there.

But the simple thought of returning to the Big Smoke was enough to get her hackles up, to put her in mind of a cat with its fur on end, its claws extended, thoroughly *rejecting* that particular idea.

But how else should she approach this?

She couldn't possibly *stay*.

When they reached her barge, Benjamin stood a few paces back, as if he had misunderstood the context of her invitation — men could sometimes be *such* idiots — and so she reached out for his hand, wound her fingers about his, and dragged him down onto the deck of the barge. Even when she'd got him sat down on one of the bench cushions, and with a glass of whisky in his hand, he refused to relax totally. He seemed wound up, as if he had his mind on something.

And — for all Lola knew — he *did*.

He peered out through one of the port windows, over the night-time water as it sent the orange streetlamps glittering in its surface. "This is a, uh, quite unusual place to live, don't you think?"

She busied herself with the record player located across the other side of the room: another one of those anachronisms; those odd little trinkets about the barge which wouldn't have fit anywhere else. From the LPs all stacked up together, she picked out one by Miles Davis. The name of it escaped her, but she would often put it on when she didn't want to think anymore . . . often after she'd had one of her feverish dreams during the day — when she wanted to get herself shot of all those thoughts and feelings, and images.

As the first notes of Miles Davis's trumpet sounded, Lola felt a slight tingle pass through her; that sense of anticipation which often gripped her just before a kill. One of the only things she *could* feel. Sometimes she wondered whether she might be more drawn to killing not only because of necessity, but in order to just feel *something.*

She glanced back over her shoulder to Benjamin.

She could see that his eyelids were drooping, and that his head was lolling on his shoulders. His grip remained firm on the whisky glass, though. The whisky within containing the sedative was not entirely drunk; not that it mattered.

A sip would suffice.

He had already drunk more than enough.

As Miles's tones drifted about the sleepy interior of the barge, she acted quickly. She headed over to the walnut dresser, slid through the drawers until she located what she had been looking for: the derringer pistol; the one which she had uncovered her very first day of inhabiting the barge, and which she had fantasised about putting to good use ever since.

It was loaded — just a single bullet — but enough to make it look like suicide.

Enough to make it look like all the others.

And to keep her tracks covered.

To keep her *secret* safe.

She gripped the pistol down by her side and approached him. As she drew close, she lowered herself down onto the bench cushion. Seeing that the tumbler of whisky was about to slip free of his grasp, she reached for it and prised it free.

She laid it down safely on the small coffee table.

For a long few moments, she held herself very still, beside him; waiting to lean forwards and suck the life force from his neck. Even looking back, she wasn't certain what it was that distracted her.

A twig snapping underfoot?

A muttered word?

Some new smell?

All she was aware of was the suddenly blinding light which flooded in through the barge windows. Shocked, she brought her forearm up to cover her eyes from the glare.

She staggered back from Benjamin's collapsed — *comatose* — body, feeling her heart fluttering up to her throat, almost choking her.

There was the stamp of feet.

There were several *thumps* at the barge door.

Thumps which shook the whole boat.

Then one final, decisive *crash* as the door caved in on itself.

Light *poured* in.

She found herself on the receiving end of a barrage of commands. All at once, she tried to do what they said . . . she was aware of allowing the gun to drop from between her fingers. Its dead weight clattered at her feet. Then she got down on her knees. Put her hands behind her head. And waited.

Waited for them to take her away.

## IV

Throughout her existence, she had been evading the police — the *authorities* — in one form or another, and she supposed that this time she had allowed herself to get sloppy; to get comfortable, in this quiet university town. That was the thing about vampires, they had to keep on moving. Never stop. Because stopping meant death.

As she found herself in a prison cell, she spotted the barred window above — not much larger than a letterbox. Although there was a bunk, she decided instead to sit on the concrete floor, to press her back flat against the wall.

For the remainder of the night, she stared up at the window, waiting for her end to come. For the sunbeams to finish with her.

She closed her eyes.

---

When she felt the heat up against her skin, the sensation was almost heavenly. And she wondered if this was what it felt like to be human again. She hadn't really *realised* just how much she had missed the feeling; the sun's rays against her skin. But she would only savour this sensation for a moment, because — like her existence — it would soon be gone.

As the sunlight reddened the backs of her eyelids, she waited for the pain to kick in — she waited for the *tearing* sensation which she had always imagined, the unimaginable *ripping* of her skin as the sun cut her to the bone.

But it didn't come.

Confused, she opened her eyes, blinked against the glare from the sunlight pouring in through the window above. She blinked again. Waited. But the end simply wouldn't come. The sunlight wouldn't do away with her.

Was this some sort of joke?

Was someone playing a *joke* on her?

As she sat back against the wall, there was the *jangle* of keys outside her cell, followed by the meshing of the locking mechanism. A *bleep-bleep* indicated that some key card, or fingerprint, or whatever they used, had been accepted.

She stared hard at the opening door, and then took in the person who stood in the doorway.

*Benjamin.*

The policeman who had taken her out for a drink.

The policeman who . . . she had tried to *devour.*

This time he didn't wear a uniform.

His baggy suit concealed his wiry frame.

He gave her a slight smile, a mock salute, tapping his forehead, and then wandered inside. The door swung shut automatically behind him.

He sat down on the bunk opposite, and clutched his hands together. He pointed to the sunlight dribbling in through the window. "Thought I'd give you a room with a view."

She shook her head, stared at him — *beleaguered.* "I . . . I don't . . ."

"The least I could do." He arched his back, shrugged his shoulders and then stretched his arms up to the ceiling. "It's not every day that you have the privilege of being a prospective murder victim."

" 'Murder victim' ?" Lola replied. "But, I . . . I *needed* to . . . I would have died if I hadn't . . . I . . ."

Benjamin raised his eyebrows, as if he dared her to continue.

Another thought struck her. "Your real name's not Benjamin, is it?"

He shook his head.

"And you don't live with your mother, do you?"

He quickly crossed himself, and then gave her a beaming grin. "Poor old Mum, she's been dead for a good ten years now."

"But . . . I . . ."

"Listen," he went on, "this is what's going to happen. In about half an hour a vehicle's going to arrive to take you to a more secure facility, before that happens can I get you anything to eat or drink?"

"Uh . . ."

He hoiked himself up off the bunk, went over to the door and then rapped his knuckles three times. "You let me know, okay?"

As the door levered open on its hydraulic arm, she felt something within her snap, something within her chest — something which she had always believed would remain perfectly guarded by her ribcage. "Uh, sorry . . . ?"

He lingered, one arm propping him up against the doorframe, the other hovering just above his belt buckle. "What?" he said, for the first time in their acquaintance sounding a little impatient.

"A glass of water, please?"

With a curt nod, he left her behind.

The door closed.

As she sat there, her back pressed up against the concrete wall, she felt the warming sunlight on her face. And she wondered how it had happened; how it had come to be.

How she was *human* after all.

# Footprints

# 1

Alex pulled a packet of cereal from the cupboard and poured it into a bowl. He yanked open the fridge door. "Carly?" he called upstairs. "There isn't any milk."

Footsteps sounded on the stairs and Carly entered the kitchen. "Are you sure?"

"Yeah, second bloody time this week."

She sidled up alongside him and looked inside.

He glanced at his watch. "Look, I'm late. I don't have time for this." He plumped himself down at the table and ploughed through his dry cereal.

Once finished, he whipped his jacket off the back of his chair and threw it around his shoulders. He kissed Carly goodbye then hurried out the door.

A trail of muddy footprints led from the road and up his drive to his garage. He stopped a moment to inspect them, but, seeing the bus shoot past, he had to tear himself away.

## 2

Alex arrived to work around nine and sat at his computer. The day's activities swamped over him and he let his brain zone out while he typed his way through his figures and documents. Those footprints ate away at his mind. One of these days he should clean out the garage.

At eleven, he headed for the break room. Inside, his boss Buldock and the Assistant Regional Manager, Tyson, stood with steaming mugs in their hands chatting away.

Alex slid a cup under the nozzle of the coffee machine and pressed a button.

"Did you see the game last night?" Buldock asked.

Black coffee spat into Alex's cup. He withdrew his cup and blew away the heat. "Nah, didn't have time. Got home and dropped into bed."

Buldock raised an eyebrow. "Working you too hard, am I?"

Alex laughed.

Tyson said, "You've got to take more time out for yourself. Structure your time better. Smell the roses."

"Perhaps you're right," Alex said. "Don't even have time to clean the garage." He eyed Tyson and Buldock, worried he might be putting the wrong message across. "Not that I mind it, as long as I get a decent breakfast in the morning."

"And do you?" Buldock asked, chuckling.

"Well, to tell the truth, we haven't had milk for a week."

Buldock said, "Looks like you should go about firing your milkman."

"I'm sure the old bastard will sort himself out by tomorrow."

They laughed.

Tyson, however, remained serious. He set his cup down on the table and eyed Alex. "You know, it's eerie. I read about something similar a few days ago. About milk." His eyes twitched between them.

"What'd you read?" Buldock asked.

"It was in a magazine, a real life story. There was this working man, yeah, and he would go to the office every day of the week, same time and everything, and when he woke up in the mornings the milk was never there."

"And what happened?" Alex asked.

"Well, this went on for months. He called up the distributor but they claimed they delivered every day on time. That was what was listed in their records."

Alex narrowed his eyes. "What then?"

"He gave up. Decided to buy some every evening on the way home from work so he'd have fresh milk for breakfast."

Buldock chuckled. "Not much of a story that." He held his fingers up like quotation marks. " 'The mystery of the milk that never came'."

Alex laughed along.

Tyson remained straight-faced. "One day, he came home early from work. Do you know what he found?"

"Go on," Buldock said, taking another sip of coffee.

"Found the wife in bed with the milkman."

Lightning ran up Alex's spine. "Why? How?"

Tyson said, "The blighter had been coming in late to deliver more than just milk."

Alex's muscles tensed up. "You're saying Carly might be pulling something like that on me?"

Both Tyson and Buldock were serious now. If there was one rule at the office, it was never to laugh when another man's wife was involved. Buldock cleared his throat. "If you want to head off home to check, I'd be happy to let you. No problem."

Could it be true, his Carly with some . . . *milkman*?

Alex swallowed. "Thanks, I'll send you the finished accounts this evening." He threw his cup in the bin and marched out, grabbing his jacket on the way.

## 3

On the bus journey home, he ran through the possibilities. If he got home and Carly was in bed with the milkman, what would he do?

He'd probably scream at her, but then what?

Perhaps he should've asked someone to come with him so he wouldn't do anything he'd regret.

Back home, he trotted up the drive. The footprints were still there. It gave him an idea. He'd surprise them, not give them the pleasure of an advance alert by having him open the door.

He ran his fingers under the garage door and lifted.

It creaked up.

Inside a half decomposed body hung from the roof.

Blood dripped into crimson puddles.

It was the milkman.

Beside him Carly held his arm in her mouth.

Alex's stomach wrenched and he vomited.

Carly stepped away from the body and stared at her feet, as if ashamed.

# GhostMail

As always seems to be the case these days, I found myself slipping away as the train pulled into London Euston Station, my mind drifting onto . . . *other* matters.

It was any wonder that I had the presence of mind to grab a takeaway coffee from one of the stands on my way out of the station.

But I did.

Addiction's a funny thing.

A subconscious *nudge*.

As I slurped back the bitter, creamy froth, I felt the morning sun beat down on my jacketless shoulders. It was something of a novelty that I didn't need a jacket before eight thirty on this fine, summer, Monday morning. And one which I was determined to take full advantage of.

At the office, I took the stairs instead of the lift, reasoning with myself — as I did every morning — that it negated the need for a gym membership. Not that my forty-year-old's beer gut is any sort of ringing endorsement for that argument.

As I crossed the office floor of *Snappy Designs*, a few drops of coffee trickled down the side of the paper cup and onto the leg of my newly bought trousers. The ones I'd bought for my grandmother's funeral a week ago.

On my way to the corner office I'd fought for twenty years to obtain, I grabbed a couple of napkins off a stack precariously balanced beside the water cooler. That done, with my coffee cup, briefcase and jacket in one hand, I used the other to dab at the white splodge that'd been left behind.

I cast a quick glance across the office cubicles.

Nobody had arrived for work yet, of course.

That was the thing about working here.

Mornings were *really* quiet.

Almost as if none of the grunts had any sort of *passion* for their work.

That thought pinned a grim smile on my face, but it was wiped off only moments later when, only a matter of steps from crossing the threshold into my office, something caught my eye. There, half-visible above my cheapo, pinewood desk, I made out a bald head. As I took another few steps, actually entered my office, I saw that the man was on his knees, dressed in worn-out, blue overalls. He had on those plastic kneepads to avoid strain acting on his, well, kneecaps.

On the floor beside him, he had open one of those bashed-up, multi-level toolboxes: one of those defining accessories of manliness.

But despite this subtle show of masculine strength, I decided to take a chance.

The man's overalls seemed to *hang* off his skeletal frame.

And, to top it all off, he was a good couple of decades older than I was.

Yes, I was reasonably confident that, if it came to it — *God forbid* — I could take him in a fight.

Still gripping my coffee cup, briefcase and jacket in one hand — the napkins in the other — I cleared my throat. "Uh, excuse me, can I help you?"

The man, having ducked down below my desk, came up with a *thump!*

He'd whacked his head on the underside of the desk.

I winced a little, tilted my head down to him. "Are you all right?" I said.

Gripping the top of his — rather red and flaking — scalp, the man emerged from beneath the desk. He wore a pair of thin-framed glasses which seemed to amplify his pupils by factors of a hundred. He was grimacing — in pain, apparently.

When I judged that he wasn't going to need an air ambulance, I changed my tone. "What're you doing here, in my office? Who let you in? Was it Toby, Juana" — I paused for a long few seconds, then arched an eyebrow — "Vanessa?"

I made sure to *hiss* the *s's* of Vanessa's name to make it clear to him that, if he was to just give me the word, he would be absolved of everything in a click of the fingers. It had been one of my most recent campaigns to get *rid* of Vanessa: what with her airy-fairy memory when it came to passing on missed calls; how she was *constantly* tapping away at her phone on some godforsaken *chat* app; the *unprofessionally* low-cut tops she enjoyed wearing and which, it was my secret belief, had got her foot in the door with my colleagues who had interviewed her.

The man, though — the *technician* — didn't seem to get the hint.

He scowled at me. "Got the keys in the post, just like we always do, mister." He nodded to my desk where, sure enough, there was a spare key to my office.

For some reason, the fact that the key had no key ring, no tag attached to it, made it seem somehow naked.

I turned back to the man, who was now bent over his toolbox, putting his tools away, his work apparently nearing its end. "Come now," I said, "*who* sent you the key in the post — and, more to the point, *why* did they send you the key?"

The man feigned not to hear me . . . or maybe he *didn't* hear me: old people are often too proud to get their hearing tested, much less to wear a hearing aid.

He slapped the top of his toolbox shut, and then rubbed his hands up against the sides of his overalls as if he was cleaning them. Still *ignoring* me, he heaved his toolbox up and laid it down on my desk.

I had to sink my teeth into my lower lip to avoid giving the man a tongue-lashing.

*Just* who *did he think he was?*

From somewhere, the man produced a clipboard — an *actual, real-life* clipboard, with a page attached to it and everything. "Sign here, please," he said, pointing to a dotted line at the bottom of a whole page of miniscule text.

I squinted at the page, remembered myself — remembered *whose* office I was standing in — and laid my briefcase and jacket down on the chair by the door, opposite my desk: the one which I'm most used to observing job applicants or staff members facing disciplinary action *squirm* in.

I held onto my coffee cup, the addict in me saying that there was still one last, good slurp puddled in the bottom. "Look here," I said, making eye contact with the hapless technician. "I'm not signing anything until you tell me what this is all about, and who abetted your breaking into my office."

I held firm, kept his too-big pupils fixed with my own.

Finally, the technician nodded back to the form on the clipboard. "All the information is there, sir." He jerked his head around to read the form upside down. "Ms M Tidsdale," he said, and then looked back at me. "She's the one who ordered this done."

I felt my blood freeze in my veins.

My heart stopped for several seconds, and then — the caffeine kicking in, I guess — skittered back into its uneasy, choppy pace. "I beg your pardon."

The technician fixed me with a hangdog expression. "Please, sir, just sign off on the job, then I can leave you in peace."

Over my shoulder, I was vaguely aware of people arriving to the office. There was a little *chatter* in the air. People talking about their weekends. All those high spirits which accompany 'free' time still floating about without being kept in check.

Nothing like a week at the grindstone to sort *that* out.

I looked over the page, glanced up to the address at the top.

Sure enough, my *grandmother's* address.

Her name, of course, was Ms M Tidsdale — *Mary* Tidsdale.

I glanced back over my shoulder, and, seeing one of the grunts looking in, I kicked the door shut with a deft flick of my back heel. It didn't make a slam as I had hoped, but only whispered — *anticlimactically* — shut.

I turned on the technician, who now held his head to one side, as if *I* was the one making trouble for him. I kept my voice even — *strong* — and didn't take my eyes off him for a moment. The Art of the Reprimand is *all about* the eyes.

"I don't know *who* put you up to this, but I'm calling you out, all right?" I stepped over to my phone, doing what I should've done right from the start. I picked it up, held the handset to my ear, already hearing the *buzz* of the dial tone. My finger hovered over *zero*, the number which would connect me to the building security.

"I wouldn't do that if I were you, Mister Freedly."

"No?" I said, glancing up, seeing those inky black pools staring out at me from beneath the thick lenses. "And why not?"

"Because, Mister Freedly," the technician went on, "Ms M Tidsdale — your *grandmother* — knows all about the company money you've been stashing away in offshore accounts."

It was then I felt those symptoms my doctor warns me about every yearly check-up:

Chest pains.

Dizziness.

Shortness of breath.

And . . . oh yes, a chilly sweat breaking out from beneath the back of my shirt.

As I felt myself bending at the knees, collapsing down into the chair by the door — falling down on top of my jacket and briefcase — I just about managed to say, in a reedy, weak voice, ". . . Get out . . . get *out* now . . ."

The technician sighed, clamped hold of his toolbox and then handed me over the clipboard. He even had the grace to hand me over a pen too.

I glared at him for several moments and then I signed on the dotted line.

For the first time, the technician smiled. From somewhere he produced a baseball cap — the same blue as his overalls — and thrust it down over his bald head. As he sauntered out of my office, I managed to get a look at the logo on the front:

*GhostMail*

---

If I'd had a shred of strength, I would've throttled the technician before he could've got halfway across the office. There seemed to be endless reasons for my doing so: the first, how he had broken into my office, uninvited, and fiddled about; the second, how he had implored me to sign that *ghastly* form of his — of which he had left me behind a carbon copy; the third, how he hadn't closed the door to my office behind him on his way out, and so had left me, clutching at my chest, flattened in the Chair of Humiliation, being observed by anybody who cared to cast a glance in my direction.

Before anyone had a chance to take a picture, I slammed my office door shut with a well-aimed kick. This time it did *slam*.

I managed to stagger my way out of the chair by the door, and made it back behind my desk without further incident. It was a rare case of reason overruling chemistry as I observed what remained of my cup of coffee. Without a second thought, I tossed it into the bin in the corner of my office.

For about ten minutes, I sat at my desk, reclining, breathing in deeply, and then out again, calming myself down. When I felt my heart tapping back away at somewhere approaching its normal rhythm, I glanced over at the carbon copy. I swivelled it around on my desk and glanced over the fine print.

Although I would've had to take a trip down to Legal to thrash out all the nuances of the thing, I could make enough of the document to understand the basics.

And yet, to me, it seemed like something out of a police procedural drama.

What the document facing me declared was nothing less than the ability to make certain 'adjustments' to my lines of incoming, and outgoing, communication.

A *wiretap*?

Towards the bottom of the document, in the paragraphs near the end, there were certain, quite specific threats. The most prevalent of these was the threat that, if I failed to comply with this written ruling, if I attempted to interfere with the device — or *devices* — which'd been fitted to my computer and telephone, then following the morning of the 'sabotage' a large paper binder would be sent up to my office. Although the details of the contents of this binder were hazy, at best, it was implied that it would be nothing less than explosive.

In short, the contents of the binder would *ruin* me.

As I leaned back in my chair, staring through the slatted blinds, out across the office floor, I thought back to what the technician had said. How he had said that my grandmother had *known* of my financial activities. What he had hinted at had been *far* too specific to have been a mere fluke. He had to have some inside information.

And there was only one place where he might've obtained it.

I reached for the phone, dialled, then thought better of it.

I replaced the handset in its cradle.

Stared at the beige plastic as if it might leap up and slash me across the throat.

I got up from my chair, grabbed hold of my jacket and dipped my hand into the inside pocket, producing my phone from within.

After glancing about, as if I might see a giant microphone sitting on my desk, I slipped out through the door, and across the office floor.

As I went, I called out to my assembling staff, "Heading out for five minutes — if you need anything it can wait till then."

Despite this statement, I found myself facing up to Emma — dear, *China-doll* faced, *Emma*. Those sparkling, clear blue eyes stared out at me from those curtains of black hair which framed her complexion. If it had been any other employee I would've shouted them down in a second, made a spectacle in front of the whole office. But since it was Emma, I fed her something approximating a smile, and said, "Not now, dear, busy," pointing to the phone I held to my ear.

---

I leaned up against a tree in Regent's Park, near to the Open Air theatre, my phone pressed to my ear. If anybody was trying to bug me then they'd have to be pretty determined to go wiring up the whole park, so I thought myself more or less safe.

"What'd you mean Alex isn't there?" I said, having caught my accomplice — *Alex's* — secretary. I listened patiently for the response. "Well when's he gonna be back?" I didn't much like that response at all. "Of course I've *bloody* tried him on his mobile! This isn't the nineteenth century, don't you think that's the first thing I did?"

Alex's secretary hung up.

I felt my chest tighten and it took a great deal of restraint *not* to toss my mobile off into the bushes.

I told myself to breathe in deeply, stared out across the greenery of the park.

It wasn't like Alex to be late for work — he was even more of a stickler for time-keeping than I was. There were times when he'd call me up at six in the morning, while I was still in bed, and crow at me about how beautiful that particular morning's sunrise was.

*Bastard.*

I wondered what was next, what I should do.

I checked my watch. It was a few minutes before nine.

Feeling my heart skip more beats, I breathed in deeply, right to the pit of my lungs.

Then I breathed out again.

I shook my head at the park stretched out before me: the twittering birds, the sweet-smelling grass, the warm sunlight which *poured* down . . . it seemed like it had to be a joke that today, of all days, the most beautiful day of the year, everything was going to come tumbling down.

My *life* was going to come tumbling down.

---

Back in the office, I got a call at about ten o'clock, right as I was about to go into a meeting. It was Alex's secretary. She informed me that he'd just called in. He'd told her in a panicked — yet *succinct* — manner that he was 'fleeing the country', in his own words. He'd then given her a series of instructions related to certain paper records, and digital records in his office. Why his secretary had thought to ring me before acting was another matter entirely — indeed, my manners with her earlier on shouldn't have left her willing to do me any favours. But, needless to say, I was polite to her *now*.

I asked her if she wouldn't kindly mind letting me in to 'find something I'd left behind' before she set into Alex's documents.

She agreed.

A few phone calls later, I managed to cancel said meetings and skip across town to Alex's office. When I got there, I almost came to blows with the security man on the door. He seemed to take exception to my face.

Despite Alex's supposed hurry to flee the country, his office was still in fairly good order. I brushed in through the flimsy metal door, which would've looked more at home in some arch villain's bunker, and I immediately set about rifling through Alex's drawers, not bothering about leaving the office in the same state which I had found it.

As I madly scrambled about, I noted Alex's secretary standing in the doorway, watching me closely, her fingers held up to her parted lips. A couple of times, she made little *peeps* — not even fully realised *noise* really — but I silenced her all the same with a quick glare over my shoulder.

When I'd got through with turning Alex's office upside down — from top to bottom — I turned on his secretary. Apparently seeing me coming, that my rage would soon turn onto her, she attempted a retreat, but I acted quickly, snatching her by the wrist.

"Tell me," I said, "has there been anybody else here? Anybody apart from Alex?"

For a long few seconds, I was certain that the secretary was going to faint . . . but then, with a couple of blinks, she seemed to bring herself back around. She stared back into my eyes, kept her voice gentle and steady, then said, "A man — a *bald* man . . ."

I clenched her wrist tighter still. "When? When did you see him?"

"He left about five minutes before you arrived."

I released her, dashed out through the doorway, feeling my heart beating against my ribs. When I got to the door to Alex's office, I remembered myself, and looked back to her. From somewhere, I managed to raise a smile — one of those *half-polite* deals I can force out of myself if, say, faced with an hours-long flight with an 'adorable' toddler sat beside me.

"Thanks for your help," I said, and then curtly slipped out into the street.

---

I spotted the white van right away.

It was parked up about thirty, forty paces from the front door of Alex's office building.

That same logo for 'GhostMail' emblazoned on its side.

Although I could hear my heart hammering in my ears, the sweat drooling down between my shoulder blades, I played it cool. As I trod along the pavement, I felt the harsh, mid-morning sunlight against my skin. What had been — this morning — a very pleasant warmth had now turned into something approximating a baking-hot oven.

When I reached the white van, I rapped my knuckles against the driver's window.

As I peered inside, I could see that the bald man from that morning — the one who had been in my office — was sat at the wheel. He was chomping on a bacon butty . . . I knew because I could smell the salty fried fat even out there, on the street.

I did my best to put on a reasonable expression, which was more easily said than done seeing as my heart was still squirting along at several hundred clicks per minute, and my whole body seemed to have become locked in an unstoppable shaking.

The bald man brought his sandwich down from his lips, turned his head slightly.

Brought me into focus with his black eyes.

He didn't seem surprised to see me.

He wound the window down just far enough so that — if I had really wanted — I might've been able to get a couple of fingers in.

Then again, I supposed, from my behaviour that morning, he had every right to exercise some caution around me.

"Please," I said, sounding far more desperate than I'd wanted to, "can you tell me what this is all about? Why you're doing this?"

The bald man continued to regard me with his stony expression. He held his bacon butty tightly in his fist, and I could see that a dollop of ketchup was sliding free from the white bun.

"Please," I repeated, as if this might loosen him up.

And, as a matter of fact, it did.

The lock on the door clicked open.

I reached out and pulled the handle towards me.

Then, with a nod from the bald man, I hauled myself up onto the passenger seat. As I sat there, my heart beating away in my throat, the sweat beading down my face, I could hardly keep it together.

But the bald man was in no rush.

He took another few bites from his bacon butty, finishing it up, and leaving a smudge of ketchup on his chin. When, with a nervous smile, I tried to indicate this remnant to him, the bald man wiped at the opposite side of his mouth, and I didn't have the energy to tell him again.

The bald man fully wound down the driver's window and stared out across the street, to the tidy park just across the road. "Whatcha want to know?" he said.

I felt a quiver pass through my gut. I steadied myself. "I want to know *why*."

The bald man, the back of his head pointed towards me now, gave a vague nod. "They always want to know *why*." He paused for the longest time, as if he was sorting through a pile of mental prompt cards. Still with the back of his head towards me, he continued, "Your grandmother knew you were stealing from her —"

I had to cut in there.

"I *wasn't* stealing from her, she signed off on the forms. I *explained* it to her."

The bald man turned back to me. His eyes met mine. A wry

smile appeared on his face. "You explained it to her when she was no longer in a position to say yes or no, you bided your time, waited till she would be just giddy enough that she wouldn't have the first idea of what she was signing."

Although I wanted to say something in response — wanted to *defend* myself — I knew that I couldn't reasonably do so . . . at least not on *those* lines.

"Look," I said, trying for another angle, "I did it for her own good — it was a good system, a way to grow her savings — "

"An *illegal* means of growing her savings," the bald man responded, his pupils like a pair of oily pits.

Again, that left me speechless.

The bald man continued to stare at me, waiting for something else. When it became apparent that I had nothing else at all to say, he broke off his gaze, peered out through the windshield, to the flawless day outside.

A pair of children — screeching with laughter — padded on past the white van, their mother pushing a pushchair behind them, laughing also.

A void opened up within my chest.

The bald man spoke to me in a low drawl. "You'll get the same deal they all get."

"And what deal's that?"

The bald man glanced back at me for a moment, sniffed as if he might have some sort of allergy. "Back when your grandmother signed up for our service — for us to keep an eye on her affairs if she should become incapacitated mentally — she designated a group of charities into which she would like such moneys to be deposited."

I screwed up my eyes. " 'Charities?' " Although I hadn't consciously intended it so, the word came out almost as a curse. I attempted to correct myself. "Why didn't she just choose to leave her money to those *charities* in the first place, when she was making her will?"

The bald man smiled again. He gave a slight shake of his head. "Because she wanted to see what kind of people her grand-children would turn out to be . . . she wanted to give them the *option* of being honest." He arched an eyebrow. "You have a sister, correct?"

I nodded.

"Yes," the bald man continued, "she shall be quite nicely served by the inheritance — you have no need to worry about her. In your case, though, it's not quite as . . . uh, *straight-forward*."

I felt as if every muscle in my body had seized up.

My heart beat in double time.

Sweat seemed to ooze out of every pore.

"You mean," I replied, "if I'd only . . . only . . ."

"Waited?" the bald man broke in, glancing at his wrist watch. He looked back at me. "Yes, if you'd only waited until your grandmother had been pushing daisies you would've had your hands on something — not *all* of it . . . not *all* that you took from her — but *some* of it. A fair share."

There was a tingling feeling all through my blood.

I started to shake my head, though I couldn't understand *why* . . .

"Now," the bald man went on, again glancing to his wrist watch, "I've got another appointment within the hour." He looked to me. "Let's talk through your options, shall we?"

---

Considering the circumstances, considering what I might've had to lose if the bald man from GhostMail had turned me over to the authorities, I got a good deal.

He informed me that I could either turn over all the money which I had accumulated using my grandmother's savings so that it might be 'redistributed' according to her wishes, or he could hand over all the information GhostMail had gathered on me to the authorities.

I chose the former option.

When I asked after my partner — *Alex's* — role in all this, the bald man gave a slight chuckle and shook his head. He told me that the two of us would go 'free' as long as we agreed to wire all the money in our names to GhostMail.

As I stood on the curb, outside my office, all the necessary phone calls made, and all the appropriate financial wheels spinning, I glanced back to the bald man, sat behind the wheel of his white van. He wore a slight smile, and I realised that I *had* to ask him.

"Is it just you — just you working alone?"

The bald man reached over to the passenger side of the van, undid the glove compartment and — from what seemed to be a sizeable stack — he slipped out a business card.

Simple.

Ivory-white.

The GhostMail logo stamped onto the reverse side.

The bald man sat up straight, adjusting his seat belt, and then one of the wing mirrors. He spoke to me out of the corner of his mouth, his withered fingers resting on the key in the ignition. "You'd be surprised how many of us there are — we're all around, really." He glanced back at me, gave me a nod, then saying, "Good luck," he started the engine.

He left me standing there, on the curb, the card for Ghost-

Mail clutched firmly between my fingers. As I watched his van roar off around the corner, heard the twittering of the birds, the *clack-clack* of high heels against pavement, I eyed a rubbish bin a few paces away.

I screwed up the business card for GhostMail in my fist, made to release it into the bin — *forgotten forever more* . . . but, as I was ready to let it drop, something stopped me.

Now, I don't believe in ghosts — none of that nonsense — but it was as if a hand gripped tight to my fingers, refusing to allow them to go slack.

I drew my hand back out from the slot on the rubbish bin, glanced at the card again.

And I slipped it into the breast pocket of my shirt.

I never knew when I might need it.

# Blood At Night

# 1

S*izzle! Boom! Cheer!*

*Sizzle! Boom! Cheer!*

*Sizzle! Boom-Boom! Cheer!*

What the hell was it about fireworks that got Justin's goat so much?

It wasn't like they were the signal for a war about to grind into action, no firing on enemy soldiers, nothing like that, though he could still remember clearly the sounds of wartime explosions. All around. All the time. Trembling up through the ground.

And if it wasn't that — some sort of an attack on his post-traumatic stress disorder — then there seemed to be only one simple explanation.

That there were people — out there — that wanted to have fun.

And, for some reason, more than anything else, that annoyed him all the more.

Oh, he knew that he should've been happy to hear even the tiniest of stirrings of life to remind him that, out there, beyond the threshold of his porch, there was still a world.

People going to work, kids going to school, teenagers getting drunk, that sort of thing.

All those things that he had got up to.

But he couldn't help but feel mightily pissed off at it all.

As he sat up on the edge of his squidgy mattress — its springs now so worn down as to resemble nothing more flexible than a plank of wood — he shovelled his toes into his slippers. Felt that familiar, woolly warmth about his otherwise bare feet.

He gave a cough, felt it rattle his ribcage, and he caught that bloody taste at the back of his mouth. He swallowed it back down with the aid of a sip from the glass of water which he kept on his bedside table, and then he rocked himself to his feet, almost like a tree taking root in one of those sped-up videos they sometimes showed on the television.

*Bam!*

Another one.

Another firework.

He wondered if he was supposed to feel a chill running down his spine, or the crunching of his gut. But, in truth, he felt nothing at all. And why should he have done? He'd never been afraid of explosions his entire life, so why should he start now?

No, the only thing that sent that chill running through him were those joyful cheers of the people in the park nearby — because surely that was where they were — busy setting off the fireworks this Saturday night.

He reached about, down to the foot of his bed, and he retrieved his dressing gown — a new one which his grandkids had got for him for his latest birthday, or had it been the year before, or the year before that? That was the thing with birthdays. At his age, they just didn't seem to be important any longer.

Replacing his glass of water, he looked to the neon-red display of his digital alarm clock — which was, as always, set to six the next morning — and he saw that it had just gone half ten at night.

He shifted his gaze to his cheap telephone which sat there at the side of his bed, and then he looked to the card he kept always tacked to the wall — the number of his local community police officer:

Carol.

A woman.

But a *severe* woman.

He then looked down even further, to the socket in the wall, and to the cord of the phone which lay on the carpet: disconnected.

If there was one thing that he abhorred above other people having fun, it was having a phone chirrup in his ear past eight o'clock in the evening when he was all tucked up in bed with a good book, lost in those imaginary worlds, in different times; times far, far . . .

*Sizzle! Boom! Cheer!*

He crunched his fingers into fists, and then lurched downwards, feeling his muscles all draw themselves into tight — warning — knots, and then he plugged the phone back in.

Another couple of seconds later, he heard the gentle *purr* of the dial tone. He waited patiently, lightly tapping his finger against his exposed, pock-marked thigh — looking at the purple-and-blue veins beneath the paper-white skin.

## 2

Carol wouldn't have anything to do with it.

That much became clear to Justin about three seconds into the telephone call.

It was almost as if she knew him well enough to read — or think she could read — his mind.

But, well, in this case she'd been proved right, because she'd known right away that he'd been calling about the fireworks. After all, she only lived a few roads over. She'd gone on to tell him that they had permission till eleven o'clock, that he wasn't to ring back till then . . . if he was to ring her back at all.

Though Justin had had the urge to pound the phone back down into its base, to listen to that unsatisfactory-sounding *clack* of plastic on plastic, he held himself back.

He had learned to control his temper, even if it did throb within his veins twenty-four hours a day. He supposed that had been one of the virtues instilled in him back in the Service.

A virtue extremely useful — if not necessary — for surviving peacetime.

Still, Justin was furious.

Smashed phone or not.

He launched himself up, grabbing hold of his dressing gown cord and tightening it into a knot about his waist.

What would he do now?

What *could* he do now?

He had done the calling-people-up thing . . . that was what always seemed to be expected in civilian life, to hand over responsibility for some other, neutral, party to take care of — to leave it in their hands to decide whether or not there was an issue to be dealt with at all.

Fireworks.

What was it?

Was it really those people all cheering away — those joyful explosions?

One thing was for certain, his blood was frothing through his veins, and he felt like his head might blow up from the pounding sensation he had at his temples.

The thought of the rifle he kept in the airing cupboard occurred to him right away.

In fact, he almost didn't have time to think things through before he found himself pawing his way past a stack of folded-up sheets, and reaching for the combination lock for the cupboard.

Gently, he unhooked his rifle, hanging up inside.

He looked it over, went through his routine — the same one that he'd had so engrained into him in the Service, and which, even now, stuck with him.

Then he breathed in deeply, right to the bottom of his lungs.

Out again.

A cleansing exhale.

He could still feel his pulse hammering at his temples and he knew that he simply had to do something to release the pressure. And, from experience, blood at night was just about the only thing that could help him now.

Down at his front porch, he shrugged on his thick winter's jacket, jettisoned his slippers for a pair of Wellington boots, and then, finally, drew a beanie hat down over his bald, flaky scalp, and he felt the warmth just ooze right through him.

As he reached up for the front door latch, felt its weight buckle slightly, he caught a glimpse of himself in the mirror. All dressed in black. He looked so old . . . all leathery, all wrinkled, how had it ever come to this?

He supposed that — one day — it'd just snuck up on him.

Or, more likely, it had come at night.

Left him for dead.

*Aging*, he thought, as he pressed down on the latch of the front door, and barrelled on out into the night, illuminated only by the luminescence of the streetlights and the moon.

## 3

Justin stalked along the pavement, keeping himself close to the hedges.

He held his rifle pointed to the ground as he strode onwards, knowing that his whole street — most of them elderly and living alone like him — would be tucked up in bed. And, in any case, if one of them did happen to look out of their windows, peek their noses out through their curtains, that, in this half-light, they could make themselves believe just about anything at all.

Oh, they might call up Carol, tell her that somebody had been wandering about at night with a gun . . . and, of course, Carol knew that he had a gun himself . . . but some statement from one of these frightened and alone old biddies certainly wouldn't be enough for the police to make anything stick.

Just like had happened before, when they'd seen him, when they'd called, Carol would come to the door, he would offer her a cup of tea, and then he'd show her up to where he kept his rifle locked away in the airing cupboard.

With that coating of dust always seeming to cover up the combination dial.

He recalled the one time when she'd floated the possibility of him giving his gun up, but he'd nipped that idea in the bud fairly sharpish — stated in no uncertain terms that if she really wanted to get him to give up his gun then she would need to pry it from his Cold Dead Fingers . . . and even then he reckoned that his corpse would put up a decent enough fight.

As Justin turned the corner, he checked out his surroundings.

There was nobody else about.

This was a quiet village, after all, and nobody much bobbed about in the evenings — most were tucked up watching television, or already sleeping.

Even on a Saturday.

Except for those in the park.

Enjoying the fireworks.

He looked on a little further along the road, saw the chain-link metal fence which announced the circumference of the car park.

Even from here, a good twenty paces away, and with only a little light, he could see that it was packed with cars. He strode on, his brain ticking, working out how he would get his own back, how he would make this thing go to plan . . . was there even a plan at all?

As he closed the distance, approached the gap in the fence which led into the car park, he halted. Felt that tingle run about the cusp of his neck. That feeling that somebody might be watching him. When he looked up, gazed about, trying to find the source of the irritation, he saw a kid on the other side of the road.

He wore a tracksuit, had a baseball cap tugged right down over his face, steeping it in shadow. His hands were shoved into his pockets, and Justin could see that the boy was quietly masticating, his jaw — like a cow chewing on cud — moved from one side to the other in that gentle, and never-ending, rotation.

He propped himself up against a brick wall, one of his shoes leaning back at an angle in that 'cool' way Justin had observed adolescents do.

The boy kept on staring at him.

Though Justin had no idea why.

When another firework popped above their heads, and a

sprinkling of neon-pink glitter burst out from it, lighting up the overcast sky, the boy nodded in his direction. "Tha' a gun?"

The boy had one of those, rather irritating, glottal stops — that refusal to pronounce t's . . . that was another thing which had tormented Justin throughout his life and, it seemed, it was going to torment him for just a little while longer.

Justin bowed his head, glanced out ahead, to the park, and to all the people gathered there, faces turned a shade of orange by the embers of the bonfire which smouldered away before them.

He turned back to the kid, saw that he was still in the same position, hands stuffed in pockets, apparently waiting for someone or something.

"Shouldn't you be in bed?" Justin said.

"Shun't *you* be in bed?" the boy shot back.

Justin held still. He could feel his heart making that sort of murmur that it did when he'd 'exerted' himself, as his GP would've put it. He could feel that a chilly sweat had broken out over his face, and he felt a sneeze stirring at the back of his throat.

But he held it off.

That was another thing the Service had taught him.

Total dominium over his own body.

Anything less could get him — and his brothers in arms — killed.

The boy remained leaning there, up against the wall, and then, far too casually to be anything other than intentional, he glanced from side to side, checking the coast was clear, and crossed the road, headed on up to Justin.

Though Justin's gut reaction would've been to raise his rifle, to get the boy in his sights — some things from the Service just never left his mind completely — he didn't.

Some other conditioning — from peacetime, no doubt — kicked in and told him that to do so would be unacceptable under the circumstances.

The boy made no move for the rifle, and when he'd crossed the street, he stood about five paces away, his cap still covering his face with shadow, his posture lackadaisical, to say the least. "Loaded?" the boy said.

"What's it to you?" Justin replied.

The boy gave a shrug. "Ullegal, innit?"

Justin drew in a breath, surprised himself at the iciness of the air, and he thought to himself that, soon, summer would be coming to an end, that the evenings would become shorter, and then non-existent. And the mornings brief and cold.

But he liked the winter.

Liked how it forced people inside.

Allowed only the hardiest — *the strongest* — out into its frosted wonderland.

He had been one of the strongest once.

But now . . . well, now he supposed he was one of the vulnerable.

"Whatcha gonna do?" the boy said, his tone light, mischievous. "You gonna go shoot up them people, or wha'?"

Justin looked to his side, to the park, to the bonfire there, and the people all basking in its glow. Just then, he watched another few fireworks dash up into the night sky, skidding and spinning about, out of control till their explosive demise.

"Don't know," Justin said, his voice a husky whisper.

"I'd do it," the boy said, matter-of-factly. "Do it in a heartbeat."

"Why?" Justin said, his throat now dry.

The boy gave a shrug, and Justin made out a Cheshire-cat

smile beneath the visor of his baseball cap. "Be famous, if nuffin' else."

Justin found himself blinking rapidly. He felt his chest tighten. His heart quicken. The sweats came cooler, and thicker. He wondered if he was maybe having a heart attack. It was a marvel that he'd managed to reach this stage of his life without any sort of a major health crisis — but might he find himself having one now?

What was he doing?

Out here?

With . . . this?

When had he become this crotchety so-and-so?

Had it happened overnight?

Or had it been a subtle transformation, taking years and years . . . before finally dawning on him?

Because it had dawned on him now.

He was that crotchety old man, the one who — back when he'd been a kid, and they'd been out playing football in the street — would come on out with that hatpin and stick it right through their ball so that they wouldn't break any more windows, so that they wouldn't disturb any more of the clean washing hanging up to dry.

Had that been fair, or was it something crueller?

Just like what he was doing now?

Only time would tell.

The rifle now felt almost impossibly heavy in his hands, and he thought that he might drop it at any moment. If he had been anywhere else, he might've handed it over to a helpful kid . . . after he'd emptied it of shells, and ensured the safety catch was snapped firmly into place, of course.

But this kid, no.

He had a bad feeling about this kid.

So he made to turn, to turn away from the bonfire, and all the people collected about it. He could keep his crotchety ways to himself. Could keep himself stuck — locked up — in his own home. Because, maybe, that was the best place for him to be.

As he turned his back on the bonfire, he heard the kid over his shoulder. "You wha'?" he said. "Where you off to, then?"

But Justin couldn't think to reply at all.

He knew he couldn't reply at all.

For this truly unspeakable thing that he had got it into his mind to do.

It was a wonder that he had managed to get out of the house — to get here — to the park, that he'd come this far before he had snapped to his senses.

That it had taken this adolescent to bring him around.

But he was certain that he had come around now.

As he paced along the pavement, he could hear the adolescent following at his heels. "Oi!" he said. "Talking to you, ain't I?"

Justin quickened his pace. Tripped but didn't fall. He fixed his gaze on the pavement before him. Of the entrance to his cul-de-sac — he could see it now — and put the adolescent out of his mind.

But the adolescent continued to pursue him.

Apparently not wanting to be shaken off.

"Wait!" the adolescent said.

Justin went faster still, breaking into a sort of half-jog. It was tricky to raise his feet entirely off the ground, especially in Wellington boots. More than a couple of times he believed that the rubber soles of his boots had scuffed the pavement, and that he would be thrown over. But, against all odds, he remained upright.

He lumbered onwards, the adolescent still following.

Then, when Justin reached his cul-de-sac, he sensed that the adolescent had ceased to follow. He looked back, just to check, saw that he now stood on the pavement, smirking.

And then, extremely slowly, and carefully, as if it was a practised action — for all that Justin knew it was — the adolescent brought his two fingers up into a V-shape, and he held them to his eyes, as if miming that he would be watching Justin.

And Justin supposed he would be.

He would have to take care.

And keep all his crotchety ways in check.

Because this was no longer his world, it was the world of others.

And he would have no part in it.

# Once Scarred, Thrice Shy

It started as a tickle at her left cheek. And then it turned into a warmth. A pleasant *heat*. And then . . . and then . . .

The pain was unbearable.

Searing-hot.

Jaw-breaking.

All-consuming.

It jigged and jagged down Abbie's spine. Brought her skin into countless puckered goose pimples. Stole away her every last thought.

Darkness dominated.

And — as always — she never saw the face.

On instinct, she thrust her legs downward. Felt the soles of her feet meet with the waxy floor of the swimming pool. With all her strength, she pushed upward.

Broke the surface of the water.

And then the pain was gone.

When she opened her eyes, she was met by a blinding light. All around. Slowly, real-world sensations returned. She felt the sting of the chlorine in her eyes. The *smell* of the stuff in the air. The taste of it at the back of her throat.

The last sense to return was her hearing. She had got water clogged in her inner ear and she turned her head side-on to shake it free.

The world returned in all its glory.

Kids splashed all around. They let out gleeful cries while their parents watched on with a kind of anxious pleasure.

Poolside, there was no frantic activity, as Abbie had expected. She supposed she hadn't blacked out all that long. Then again, taking stock of the half-bored lifeguard, fist supporting chin, sitting on her bright-yellow chair, with her equally bright-yellow polo shirt loosely draped over the swimming costume she wore beneath, it didn't appear that Abbie had been in any real danger of being 'rescued'.

Abbie breathed in deeply. Then she sighed out. This was the first time. The first time she had blacked out while swimming. Did that mean that the episodes were getting worse? Did that mean that she had to take more care? That, from now on, it would be reckless to permit herself to leave the house without a chaperone?

Still, perhaps it *would* be a good idea to ask either one of her triplet sisters — Allie or Annie — to accompany her. At least when she went swimming . . .

Abbie reached up to her soaking, auburn, shoulder-length hair and pulled it down over the left side of her face to conceal the scar which ran from the corner of her lip to her earlobe. She swam over to the pool steps, navigating the thrashing, giggling children, and hauled herself up and out. As she grabbed her towel and headed for the women's changing rooms, she caught the lifeguard's eye.

The lifeguard gave her a slight flash of the eyebrows. A gentle shake of the head. Her shoulders rose and fell with a sigh.

Abbie smiled back politely then left the pool behind.

---

Back home, as always, things were manic.

Abbie had hardly stepped through the front door when she heard her mother call out from the kitchen. "Abs? That you?"

Abbie didn't reply straight away. She had caught sight of

herself in the mirror, realised that she'd forgotten to apply makeup after getting changed following her swimming session. Just as it must've appeared while she was swimming, the finger-wide, deep-purple scar snaked its inevitable path across her left cheek. Where had her mind gone? She *never* forgot to wodge as much concealer over her scar as she could manage. Had that . . . *episode* . . . affected her more than she would've liked to admit?

Footsteps.

The gentle rub of slippers over carpet.

Her mother appeared in the hallway. She held a tea towel in her hands, in the middle of drying a glass. Abbie wasn't quite sure how her mother managed it, but she always seemed to appear so effortlessly elegant. Even while wearing a tracksuit and a pair of slippers. Abbie knew, from the pictures their mother had often shown her and her sisters, that she and her sisters were near carbon copies of her at their age.

*Three* near-perfect copies.

Her mother wore her sleek, auburn hair in a ponytail which bobbed and butted as she worked to dry off the glass. She smiled in an almost sickly sweet way. "Go for a dip?"

"Uh-huh," Abbie replied, dumping her sports bag down alongside the battered trainers she'd just yanked off.

When Abbie turned her attention back onto her mother, she saw that she held her head cocked to one side, as if pressing her ear up against an invisible wall. Hoping to overhear what was happening in another room. "Allie and Annie have been doing some gardening."

Abbie glanced up, looked out through the patio doors, and to the lush, green lawn beyond. Well, to tell the truth, the lawn was *usually* 'lush' and 'green' but at the present time it was covered in soil and garden implements. She saw that their dog — Socrates

— was in the middle of determinedly digging a hole, apparently inspired by Abbie's sisters' efforts. Although Abbie knew that she really shouldn't bother, she couldn't help but step past her mum and approach the glass doors. Just as her mother had claimed, Allie and Annie were down on their knees, each of them with a shawl wrapped about their hair, keeping it prim and tidy. They wore their hair in the same style as Abbie, which was to say shoulder-length.

Although Abbie would've liked more than anything else to set herself apart from her triplets — what identical siblings *didn't* have the desire to do so — she couldn't cut her hair short for fear of exposing the scar on her left cheek. And when she had intentionally grown her hair as long as she could manage Allie and Annie had done the same.

It was as if they *wanted* to look like her . . .

Before Abbie could get away from the window without attracting her triplets' attention, she heard them call her name. She glanced back, hoping to meet her mother's eye, but her mother had already returned to the kitchen.

Gone back to the washing-up.

---

Outside, the air felt starchy. Humid. Dark clouds hung above. It was a storm just waiting for a reason to break. No sooner had Abbie set foot on the concrete slabs which formed the patio than Socrates trotted up to her, eyes wide in delight, something gripped tightly between his teeth.

Although Abbie was certainly fond of Socrates, it would've been stretching things to say that she *adored* him . . . certainly not in the same way she 'adored' her cat, Spot.

In any case, Socrates was *Allie's* pet. When their mother had offered Annie a pet, she had gone with a gerbil. Socrates and Spot were still going strong some thirteen years later.

The gerbil was not.

Abbie and her sisters were now nineteen years old and while Socrates had once been jet-black with time he had sprouted grey in his muzzle and in sections of his fur. Abbie looked at the mud-clod which Socrates held in his jaws. It would be faeces of some sort — Socrates was something of an expert when it came to locating *faeces*.

She contented herself with giving him a friendly pat on the side. This seemed to please Socrates well enough and he wagged back off to his work-in-progress at the hole.

Abbie turned her attention back to her sisters, seeing that Allie was now looking over and smiling. "Putting in petunias," she said, wiping a soil-encrusted, gloved hand across her brow.

Without turning around from the current petunia she was stooped over, Annie said, "Could do with a hand if you've got a moment."

Abbie stared for a few moments at the earth, and the fledgling petunias that had already been planted. "Isn't it a bit late in the season to be planting flowers?"

Allie and Annie stopped their work.

There was a beat of silence.

Then Allie said, "What'd you mean?"

"I *mean*," Abbie replied, "that the first frost can't be far off . . . won't that just — I don't know — stop them dead?"

Neither Allie or Annie said anything.

After a few more moments, they went right back to work.

Knowing never to look a gift horse in the mouth, Abbie retreated from the garden, heading upstairs to her bedroom.

---

When she crossed the threshold, she immediately took stock of Spot lying on top of her unmade bed. As seemed to make up a good ninety-percent of his day, Spot — with his swirling, tangerine fur which brought to mind her own hair — was snoozing.

When Abbie plunged her fingers into his soft belly, giving it a rub, Spot stretched out his paws and gave a slight purr — throwing in a feline grin for good measure. He never so much as opened his eyes, but that didn't seem to matter. He *knew* it was her.

Having had her fix of cat therapy, she shifted off to her desk where she had left a book open which she'd been flipping through earlier that morning, before she'd gone out for her swim. She had no computer or TV in her bedroom. At night, she always left her mobile phone to charge downstairs on the kitchen counter (appropriately secured from prying eyes, of course). She didn't even have any kind of electronic reading device in her room. She found all that distracting. Back when she had been interested in preventing the . . . *bad dreams* . . . she had spent a lot of time researching just what environmental factors corresponded to 'good' or 'bad' sleep. And one of the factors which contributed to the latter was what was referred to in one of the advice articles as 'tech clutter'.

The open book was entitled *A Modern Introduction to Nursing*.

Just why Abbie had decided to take out this particular book from the library, she couldn't rightly say. She was due to start her History degree at the end of October, in a couple of months' time, and this 'modern introduction' would have little or no relevance to what she was going to study. But, as always seemed to have been the case for Abbie, she never merely contented herself with looking to the next year or two of her life.

She liked to keep the next decade firmly in mind.

She supposed she had picked up the book with the vague thought that she might like to train as a nurse postgraduate.

She peered down at the book now, at the page which she had left open.

It was a step-by-step guide on sutures.

Abbie supposed that, when she was first becoming self-conscious about her scar — around her pre-teen years — she had sought out all sorts of information on just *why* her face *was* the way it was. But she had soon left those areas behind, unexplored.

What difference did it make, anyway?

It wasn't like her knowing about suturing was in any way going to 'fix' her condition.

She skimmed over the pages, the images going through the work involved.

The blood in the pictures didn't bother her — blood never *had* bothered her — she was able to detach herself from what she saw. And to concentrate on the process itself.

Feeling as though she had garnered about all that she was likely *to* garner from this particular book, she slapped it shut and laid it down upon the pile.

When she glanced to the alarm clock on her bedside table, she saw that it had just gone four in the afternoon. She would need to be at the pub by six.

Her sisters, Allie and Annie, had taken full advantage of their free year before university to lie about the house during the day, tapping about on their mobile phones, watching TV, before going out on the town with their friends at night.

Abbie, meanwhile, had taken on a part-time job at a pub in

the evenings while she dedicated herself to 'getting ahead' with her forthcoming studies during the days . . . the occasional trip to the swimming pool — like today — excepted, of course.

Whenever they got around to talking about Abbie's job at the pub — and Abbie was always sure *not* to be the one to bring it up — Allie and Annie would wonder out loud just why she bothered. The insurance pay-out from their father's death four years earlier had left them *more* than enough for educational purposes.

But Abbie couldn't constrain her thinking to only the next three years of university.

Already she was focused on building up something of a savings buffer.

Money stowed away for a rainy day. And so she worked at the pub.

Feeling as though she was at a loose end, and not wanting to ruin Spot's beauty sleep, she perched on the edge of her desk chair and stared out of the window. To the clouds as they continued to gather. Did she hear raindrops beginning to strike the roof tiles?

---

It was right — *bang* — in the middle of the shift when Abbie began to feel queasy.

It was Friday night and the pub was stuffed full. The place where she worked was called *The Green Parrot* and it was located in the centre of town. The clientele was made up of almost purely office workers, and most of those male.

When Abbie had started out at the pub — about a year ago now — she had thought she'd feel intimidated by hordes of drunken *older* men. But she had soon learned the sense of fraternity which existed between herself, her fellow barmen, and — most important of all — the bouncers standing on the doors. If she ever did find herself in any sort of 'uncomfortable' situation then she had only to so much as *glance* off at Clive — the head bouncer — and he would put a stop to said situation. More often than not, it had to be said, he treated arising situations with a sense of subtlety and grace. He seldom needed to take anyone by the scruff of the neck. These people *were* here to enjoy their nights out, after all.

"Abs? You all right?"

Abbie caught Sarah — her fellow barmaid — out of the corner of her eye. She was difficult to miss. She had blond hair and bright-blue eyes. A human Barbie doll.

When the giddiness had struck, she had impulsively reached out and taken hold of the lacquered surface of the bar counter. It was only now that her senses were returning that she brought back into focus the customer standing before her. She'd been in the middle of taking an order when she'd begun to feel dizzy.

She slipped Sarah the flicker of a smile, then turned back to the customer. She felt steadier now. More *sure* of herself. She turned her attention to the task of pouring out the customer's pint and then taking his cash. The customer gave her a 'friendly' wink by way of thanks as he sauntered away from the bar.

About an hour before closing time, things got a little quieter. All of the older office men returning to their wives. The younger males headed off to a club or a late-night bar.

Abbie went off into the back room of the pub — demarcated by a beaded curtain — and started into washing glasses. She donned the rubber gloves and went to work. She hadn't been running the hot water for longer than a few minutes when Sarah appeared. She wore her familiar, gentle smile. There was something about Sarah which had always been so . . . *welcoming* . . . the two of them — over the course of the last year — had struck up something of a friendship. Sarah was currently training to become a hairdresser. During the day, she served her apprenticeship, washing scalps and sweeping up trimmings from the floor of a nearby salon. At six, she would head for the pub to put in an evening shift. Whenever Abbie asked Sarah how she didn't end every day exhausted, she would always give a nonchalant shrug and just smile.

Perhaps Sarah could teach Abbie's triplet sisters a thing or two about work.

Perhaps Sarah could teach *Abbie* a thing or two about work.

"You all right?" Sarah asked, laying down a handful of glasses with a *tinkle*.

Abbie continued to wash away, doing her best not to think about the stale smell of the ale. "Fine, thanks." Abbie waited for Sarah to go back out into the bar area, but she remained. It seemed that it wasn't going to be so easy to put an end to her concerns. If Abbie had learned one thing about Sarah throughout their acquaintanceship — *friendship*? — it was that she liked to take care of people. She wouldn't take what people said on face value. She wanted to make sure that they were *really* okay.

"It happened again, didn't it?" Sarah asked.

The current glass slipped in Abbie's grip. It shattered at the bottom of the sink. She puffed through clenched teeth.

"You know," Sarah said, "most people swear when they break a glass."

Abbie set about sweeping up the pieces of broken glass with her gloved hand. "Just force of habit."

"It *did* happen again, though, didn't it?"

Once more, Abbie chided herself for having taken Sarah into

her confidence. It had been soon after she'd started at the pub. Abbie supposed that she had been somewhat taken in by the new surroundings . . . by the fact that she wasn't at *school* anymore. It had happened one night — one night after a *long* Saturday shift. Something had snapped inside her. And Sarah had asked about her scar. In a way it had been a relief. Ever since she had started at the pub nobody had asked her about the scar. But, in another way, it had been horrifying. Because she had ended up telling Sarah about one of her innermost secrets.

One of her innermost *weaknesses*.

And the worst part? Like everyone else, they didn't *believe* her.

Sarah — just like everyone else — refused to believe that Abbie had never *seen* whoever marked her face. That whenever Abbie suffered her flashbacks during her blackouts — during her *nightmares* — she never once caught sight of the face of her attacker.

That whoever had done this to her had gotten away with it.

She had only been six years old, after all.

Abbie wasn't quite sure what she was hoping to achieve by busying herself with the broken pieces of glass. Perhaps she expected Sarah to catch the hint. And to go away. But she remained standing there. Unwilling to take her silence as any kind of answer.

The shards of glass all collected together now, Abbie cradled them in her gloved hands and dumped them on top of a newspaper someone — Terry the owner? — had left out on the side. Then she turned back to Sarah.

"Yeah," Abbie finally replied. "It happened again."

Sarah furrowed her brow. There was no trace of her smile now. Only concern. "You don't think you should go to the hospital?" Without waiting for Abbie to respond, she hooked her arm through Abbie's, and made for the back door. "Come on — I'll drive you."

Abbie allowed Sarah to escort her no more than a few steps before she stopped.

Just *stopped.*

"What?" Sarah said, turning into her. "Is it happening again?"

Abbie forced her mouth into a tight O-shape. She felt ridiculous. Still here, still wearing the rubber gloves from when she'd been washing the glasses. "I'll . . . I'll be okay."

Abbie half expected Sarah to insist.

For her to *tell* her they were going to the hospital.

Instead, though, she released her.

And a shade of the smile she'd worn returned.

"At least let me finish up those glasses for you."

Abbie took a deep breath. Composed herself. And then managed a smile and a nod. "Thank you," she replied.

---

A few days later, after Abbie had returned home from a swim, she sat up in her bedroom, once again poring over the latest batch of books she had taken out from the library. Today she *was* on message — at least where her degree subject was concerned. She was reading all about sharecropping in colonial Africa when she heard a knock on her door.

She leaned back in her chair, glanced briefly at Spot — as per usual stretched out on her unmade bed — and then asked the caller in.

It was Allie.

"Hi," Allie said.

"Hi."

Allie nodded to the desk, to the open book. "What you reading?"

Abbie had a brain freeze. She glanced back down at the pages. Before she could reply, though, Allie was wearing a sly grin.

"Must be *thrilling*," Allie said.

Abbie started to yawn and brought her hand up to stifle it.

"Look," Allie said, "me and Annie, we were just wondering, wouldn't you be interested in coming out with us?"

Having recovered from the yawn, Abbie parted her lips to protest.

But Allie wouldn't have any of it.

"Abs, we're *all* very impressed with you. You know" — she gestured at the pile of books — "the studious stuff . . . your discipline with the *job* . . . me, Mum, Annie, we all think you're an *Inspiration*."

There was a slight bite to Allie's tone.

Allie continued, "It's just . . . me and Annie think you should come out with us tonight." She broke into a Cheshire-cat, faux grin. "A night on the tiles would do you a *world* of good."

Again, Abbie attempted to intercept this offer.

But — *again* — she was cut short.

Allie took a couple of purposeful steps toward her. Then laid her hand on her shoulder in what Abbie supposed was meant to qualify as a *wizened* gesture. "You're coming out with us. It's decided."

Abbie glanced over to Spot, not for the first time envious of his perfectly solitary feline lifestyle.

---

If there was any truth to what Allie had said about Abbie being 'studious' and 'disciplined' then it could conversely be said that Abbie was lacking in other abilities.

Chief among them — at least in this context — was her ability to say *no*.

Before Abbie could so much as make a squeak, Allie and Annie had conspired to get her into a sleek, satiny, emerald-green dress which belonged to Allie. To Abbie's mind, the hem was a few centimetres too far above the knee, although she didn't dare say anything.

That might get her into *yet more* trouble.

Allie and Annie went for white and red dresses respectively.

And so here she was, sandwiched between Allie and Annie in the back seat of a taxi, as if she might be willing to make a swift escape at a moment of her choosing.

Annie had offered Abbie a nip from a hipflask she kept in her purse. Abbie had internally grimaced at herself for actually *asking* Annie what was inside. 'Water' was the reply she'd got . . . A quick sip told her this was a lie.

They arrived in town a little after eleven pm.

A light rain was falling by the time they left the taxi behind. Everything happened in a daze, Abbie absorbing the dozens of women — some her age but most a few years older — standing in line in skimpy dresses, waiting to be let into clubs and bars.

Allie and Annie apparently already had a route mapped out. They skilfully guided Abbie down several dodgy-looking back alleys and then returned to the curve of the main road. Before Abbie quite knew what was happening, they were queueing to get into a place which went by the name of *Giants*.

When Abbie trailed her sisters into the club itself she was all at once overwhelmed.

It was the volume of the music.

It was the bassline throbbing through the floor and through the walls.

How it made her gut quiver.

If it hadn't been for Annie seizing hold of her arm and leading her through the crowds, she might've become separated from her sisters there and then.

The three girls made it to the bar, where — and perhaps this was Abbie's barmaid's spider-sense tingling — she noticed them all being leered at by a nearby group of men.

Just from looking over them once, Abbie was certain they were all well into their forties. On instinct more than anything else, Abbie glanced off toward the exit of the club, as if she might see the familiar face of Clive the Head Bouncer there. But although there *was* a bouncer, he was looking off in an entirely different direction.

Just as she was doing so, she couldn't help but notice a . . . *presence* at her right elbow.

She turned to look.

A man.

One of the forty-somethings she had seen standing nearby.

*Leering.*

Sure enough, when she glanced up, she saw that the rest of his group had their gaze fixed on her. And that they all wore the same smarmy — *lecherous?* — grin.

The man wore a white shirt over a pair of tight-fitting blue jeans. He had a muscular upper body and a square jaw which told her that he surely spent a good portion of his spare time in the gym. If he was in his forties then he was at least taking care of himself . . .

His hair was jet-black and his eyebrows were like a pair of

inverted commas, drawing attention to his hazel-coloured irises. He had to lean in and shout in her ear to be heard. "Triplets. *Redheads*. Not twins?"

Abbie waited a beat, wondering if there was going to be any more to this statement. It didn't seem there would be. She looked to Allie and Annie, the two of them busy and oblivious, shouting to be heard by the barman. She turned back to the man.

It took her off guard to see him staring at her face.

Although she hadn't got a good look at his expression before, she had somehow expected him to have a grin smeared on, just like his friends. But he was . . . what was the term? . . . grave-faced. "So," he said, pointing at her cheek. "You gonna tell me about your scar?"

Unconsciously, Abbie reached up to her left cheek. She rested her fingertips on the scar. She felt faint all of a sudden. A blackness formed at the periphery of her vision. But this time she was prepared. *Somehow* she was prepared. Maybe it was her surroundings — the throbbing bass beat — or perhaps it was some deeply entrenched will for survival.

Feeling stronger now, she looked the man in the eye. She managed to raise a smile to him. It seemed the only legitimate defence. What was that about charm? About killing others with *kindness*? "What's to tell?" she replied.

"You know. How you got it." He jerked his head in the direction of Allie and Annie — they were *still* in conversation with the barman. "Or is it a birthmark or summat?"

"It's not a birthmark. Someone *cut* me."

It might've been the fact that she had to shout to make herself heard, but there was something about saying this out loud which sent a shudder passing down her spine. Although everyone noticed her scar and — in their own way — asked her about it, they didn't usually ask so directly. And she certainly never shouted out such a clear reply.

The man pouted. "He's, what, in prison now?"

"Actually," Abbie replied, seeing her sisters returning from the bar clutching a trio of drinks, "I don't know *who* did this."

Allie and Annie arrived just in time.

Allie pushed a strawberry-coloured drink in a triangular glass into Abbie's hand. "Who's this?" she asked, tilting her head into Abbie.

Abbie looked to the man again. "I didn't get your name."

"Didn't get yours."

"Abbie."

The man glanced to Allie and Annie and then seemed to slip far away. As if his thoughts had turned to somewhere altogether different.

When Abbie glanced over his shoulder to his group of friends watching on, she saw they were exchanging delighted grins and nudges to the ribs.

Finally, blinking rapidly, as if having returned from some sort of a blackout of his own, the man turned to Abbie, smiled. "Name's Rick," he said. "I've, uh, gotta go."

Abbie stood stunned as she watched Rick elbow his way through the crowded club.

She felt relieved to see him go.

Hopefully for good.

"Had a bit too much to drink?" Annie asked, leaning into Abbie's right side.

"Not got a bad pair of buns," Allie added, leaning into Abbie's left side . . . the same side which bore the scar.

Abbie wondered if Annie was right about him having 'overindulged', and that he was headed for the men's toilets.

However, instead of making for the restroom sign, he turned and left through the club exit.

First Allie pinched her.

And then Annie did.

Abbie let out an "Ow!"

"Come on," Allie said, looping her arm through Abbie's, "I didn't put my dancing shoes on for nothing, you know."

---

The start of university edged closer and closer. Abbie continued with her standard routine. Working at the bar during the evenings. Going swimming in the mornings. Doing some reading in the time between. All things considered, she believed that she'd made good use of her free year before starting into her studies.

Better use than Allie and Annie had made, in any case.

One day in the early evening, running late for work, Abbie bounded down the stairs, almost knocking over Socrates on her way — nearly kicking Spot in the face as she rounded the door to fetch her handbag she'd left on a kitchen chair. She just about had time to glance at her mother and tell her she was off to work when her mother interrupted her escape.

"Wait," her mother said, holding up an envelope.

Slowly, Abbie's gaze drifted from the envelope, along her mother's slender arm, and to her grinning mouth. Her mother arched an eyebrow. "Secret admirer?"

Right then Abbie had the urge to throw her hands up and rush out the front door. She didn't have time for this. But then, seeing the envelope wasn't addressed in any way other than with her first name — *ABBIE* — printed in careful block capitals in blue ink, she wanted more than anything to rip the envelope free of her mother's clutches.

Her mother turned the envelope over in her hands, cocking her head to one side, as if she might be able to divine something about the sender just from the outward appearance. "Pretty romantic," her mother said. "In this day and age." She glanced across the kitchen counter, to where Abbie usually left her mobile phone plugged in to charge overnight. "But, then again, I suppose you are the ultimate when it comes to playing hard to get."

Unsure whether or not she should be taking this as compliment or criticism, Abbie decided not to do either. "Mum, I'm in a rush, can we talk about this later?"

Here her mother frowned slightly. And then, seeing that Abbie was about to duck out of the kitchen, and to head off for her shift, she relented.

Something about her mother's mood seemed to shift.

It reminded Abbie of Socrates when he'd done something 'bad' and been struck smartly over the head with a rolled-up newspaper. How all the energy just seemed to *seep* right out of him instantaneously.

"Take it," her mother said, holding out the envelope. "It *is* addressed to you, after all."

Abbie hesitated a moment. And then she slipped the letter from her mother's hands.

Seeing her mother was still wearing her dejected face, Abbie lurched forward and impulsively gave her a rib-crushing hug. This wasn't at all like Abbie, who was normally standoffish at the best of times, but the situation seemed to call for the gesture.

When Abbie backed up, envelope now in her hand, and the prospect of getting out of the house seeming a more realistic proposition than it had previously, her mother fixed her with a cautious smile. "You'll be careful, won't you, Abbie?"

" 'Careful', Mum?"

Her mother said nothing more.

Abbie supposed she just had to read between the lines.

With no time to waste, Abbie bid her mother farewell and headed off to get the bus.

---

It being a Tuesday night, the pub was quiet.

Although Abbie had thought about opening the envelope on the bus ride over, the bus had been near full. Approximately thirty seconds after taking a seat, she had given it up to an elderly lady with dozens of shopping bags. And now she was at work.

Sarah was seeing to one of the few customers, taking care to pour out one of the many 'fine' cask ales the pub served. To be quite honest, Abbie wasn't sure how anybody could stand the flavour of the stuff. It was like supping on tepid water which'd been used to soak sweaty socks. Maybe it was a taste she would acquire once she'd started university.

Abbie slipped her coat off — the envelope tucked into the inside pocket — and hung it up in the back room. Then she went to join Sarah, though it didn't appear there was all that much which needed seeing to. This assumption soon proved to be a falsehood, however, when a whole group of office workers bundled in through the door.

They were celebrating a birthday — a woman who went by the name of Tracy. From her dress — prim, overly flirtatious — and her age — *young* — Abbie couldn't help thinking that she must be a receptionist. Not that she was in any sort of a position to judge . . .

The group ordered two rounds of drinks right away, as if one of the sombre regulars, supping a pint with the day's newspaper spread flat on the table before them, was threatening to do a sudden run on the pub's stock.

Sarah and Abbie worked hard to fulfil the orders as they were made — mostly ale, but with a few lager shandies thrown in for good measure. When they had finished up serving the office workers, Abbie was of half a mind to mention the letter to Sarah.

But then she saw him.

The man from the club.

The one who had introduced himself as *Rick*.

To begin with, Abbie was just flat stunned that she even remembered him. It had been a good few weeks — months? — since her sisters had dragged her along on their night-out. Aside from that bizarre episode in which she had met Rick, it had been an uneventful evening. Oh, sure, there had been dancing. And drinking. And then a *takeaway*.

But there had been nothing else which'd made it memorable other than the fact that she had met Rick in the club. And how he had excused himself then disappeared.

She hadn't expected to see him ever again.

Rick stood in the doorway for a few seconds, sizing up his surroundings. Then he cast his gaze over Abbie. And made right for her. As he approached, Abbie had just enough time to take stock of what he was wearing — a hoodie over a pair of tracksuit bottoms and trainers. She supposed that he had just come from, or was on his *way* to, the gym.

"Abbie," Rick said, propping his elbows on the bar, staring

directly at the bridge of her nose with those hazel eyes of his. "You get the letter?"

Abbie thought for a couple of moments. She was unsure how to respond. Despite the meeting with Rick being *memorable*, she had no trouble admitting — if only to herself — that she had no desire whatsoever to see him again. Let alone in any kind of *romantic* sense.

He had to be a solid twenty years older.

Albeit he looked *good* for that twenty-year difference . . .

Before Abbie had the chance to reply, Rick reached into the sports bag he carried. He unzipped one of the pockets. Produced a mobile phone. He stared at the screen, sweeping through options, and menus, and whatever else, before he came to rest on what he was searching for. He turned the phone around. Showed her the screen.

Abbie was so taken off guard that she didn't *see* what was before her eyes for the longest time. She stared at the image. The picture of the girl there.

"My cousin," Rick said. "'Bout your age, I reckon."

Sensing Sarah now standing at her shoulder, Abbie looked over the picture of the girl. She saw how there was a scar on her left cheek. Equal to her own.

*Exactly* the same.

When Abbie turned back to Rick, she saw he wore a sturdy smile. There was something reassuring about it even if this whole situation had got her feeling afraid.

No, more than afraid.

Downright *terrified*.

"Says the same as you do. That she don't remember."

Abbie looked to Sarah, and then back to Rick. There was a riotous cry from the corner of the pub. A clinking of glasses.

---

Rick hung around until the rowdy group of office workers had finally got bored and gone off to celebrate 'Trace's' birthday elsewhere. Although Abbie offered Rick a pint of something alcoholic, he asked for only a glass of orange juice. Because she thought that his pale complexion suggested he needed it, she brought him over a pack of nuts too.

Once things had calmed down at *The Green Parrot*, Abbie went over to Rick, clutching the envelope in her fist. She couldn't help noticing that Sarah was keeping an eye on her from behind the bar counter. Quite apart from feeling as if she was being mothered, Abbie was flattered and reassured by Sarah's concern. Anyway, it wasn't like they had any secrets.

Abbie had told Sarah everything she knew about her scar.

She noticed right away that Rick had left his mobile on the table, face up, with the photo of his cousin showing on the screen. It sent a fresh tingle through Abbie's blood to see the scar which matched her own.

"Opened it yet?" Rick said, nodding to the envelope.

Abbie turned her attention downward, as if the envelope had spontaneously materialised in her hands. Then, because it seemed the thing to do, she slit open the fold and removed the slip of paper inside. It was a handwritten note. The same unsteady block capitals from the outside of the envelope. All the message said was:

I WANT TO MEET TONIGHT AT THE PUB
WHERE YOU WORK.

RICK.

"I'm sure me turning up here came as a shock if you didn't read the letter. Apologies for that."

After turning the note over, and finding nothing on the other side, she glanced back up at Rick. "It's fine," she said, managing to smile.

The smile didn't stick.

Rick seemed to grasp that Abbie wanted him to get to the point. "Really don't remember, do you?"

"Remember what?"

Rick smiled. Then the smile turned to a grimace. "Don't remember my cousin? Fiona."

Abbie searched her mind. But no matter how hard she tried to know . . . she just couldn't. The information escaped her.

"Your birthday party, that's when it happened. That's where the ambulance got her from. Always said it was an accident." He shook his head, glanced back down at the photo on his phone then looked to Abbie — directly at her scar. "Things like this ain't accident."

Abbie allowed this information to dribble through her thoughts.

Her birthday party?

Did she remember anything about a *birthday party*?

Her mind continued to spin.

Sarah called out for her to give her a hand.

Abbie knew Sarah well enough to know this was Sarah's way of asking if she was okay — if she needed any help with this particular *gentleman*.

"Better get goin'," Rick said, rising from his seat, snatching his phone off the table as he went and hoisting his sports bag over his shoulder. "Missus'll be worried I'm out cruisin' the bars."

Rick had already got halfway across the pub before a thought struck Abbie.

When she spoke aloud, her voice was firm.

Much louder than she expected.

"What do you want me to do?"

Rick stopped. He turned to look back over his shoulder. Shrugged. "Jus' thought you should know. That's all. It was a long time ago. My cousin didn't say nothing concrete — never been able to. But she did say one thing. That it was two girls. Her age. Red hair. *Identical twins*."

As the pub door swung shut, Abbie felt her whole body go stiff.

And then it was as if she was sinking.

Right down into the floor.

---

Abbie got home just after midnight. She was determined that she would wait. That she would *stay up* . . . She took to reading a book on Antarctic explorers.

Somehow — amongst Shackleton and Amundsen — she found the means to keep herself awake. Waiting for her sisters to return from their night-out.

It must've been about two or three in the morning when she finally heard stirring. Footfall on the staircase. She was certain she had drifted off — just for a moment — and allowed her sisters to sneak past her, to return to their bedrooms and to safety.

But then she saw it wasn't her sisters at all.

It was her mother.

Dressed in her pearl-white, silk dressing gown her mother passed in through the doorway like some kind of wandering spirit. She held an empty glass of water clenched in her fist. Apparently she had come downstairs for a refill.

When her mother looked Abbie over, she didn't appear surprised. If anything she might've been mildly startled. But nothing more. It was as if she had been expecting to find Abbie sitting in an armchair downstairs, in the middle of the night, for a long time now.

Abbie decided to pre-empt any conversation. "You knew about Allie and Annie, didn't you, Mum? What they did to my face?"

Her mother said nothing. She simply continued to clench the empty glass in her fist.

Abbie felt a flourish of anger.

But she pushed it down.

Determined not to let it show.

Her mother pursed her lips, looked Abbie in the eye. "I didn't think you remembered."

Abbie scanned her mother's response for the longest time. Tried to understand. Desperately *wanted* to understand. And then something twigged in her mind. "You *knew*."

Her mother stared into space for a few seconds. Then she dipped her gaze. Appeared to stare at the toes of her slippers. "We wanted to wait. For Allie and Annie's sake." She glanced up. "You were all only six years old. So young. *Too* young to know. When you came around from the . . . the surgery . . . we asked you what you remembered. But you didn't remember anything."

Abbie searched her mind now. But she still didn't remember. Even though she understood the facts. Even though she now *knew* what had occurred.

She decided to turn back to what she had learned earlier that day.

"The other girl. What about her?" Abbie asked.

Her mother was silent.

This time, when the flash of anger struck, Abbie couldn't control herself. "She didn't remember either? What did you tell her parents? How did *you* get away with it?"

"Your father. He was the one who found you — both of you. He took care of the parents."

Abbie shook her head. Unable to believe. There was a long silence. Then Abbie said, "Allie and Annie never wanted me to know what happened? That *they* did this to me?"

Abbie felt a rush of emotion.

Betrayal? Helplessness? Confusion?

She looked back at her mother. "Shouldn't they know that *I* know what they did?"

"I'll leave that for you to decide."

Apparently having forgotten all about refilling her empty glass, her mother trudged back toward the staircase. She paused when she reached the first step, turning her head, looking at Abbie. "You have to understand that what happened left a scar on Allie and Annie too. Not all scars are visible." Her mother trod up the stairs.

Abbie felt a smile snake onto her face. She shook her head to herself. Felt a kind of *madness* grip her. She couldn't believe this. Simply *couldn't* believe this.

And yet it was the truth.

Of course, Abbie could see the scene playing out in her mind's eye now. What had occurred all those years ago. It wasn't a memory, of that she was sure, but it was clearly an accurate *projection* of what had occurred. The other girl . . . Rick's cousin . . . she had stumbled upon Allie and Annie . . . and what they had been doing with the knife, and Abbie's face. They couldn't just let her go.

. . . But they'd just been six years old.

How could they have known — have *really* known?

In the near distance, out in the street, Abbie could hear laughter.

Allie and Annie's laughter.

She glanced at one of the kitchen drawers.

Just briefly.

Then looked away.

That drawer — as she well knew — contained many sharp knives.

# Beyond The Blinds

Gordon listened to the coffee pot throttle away. He smelled the coffee wafting up in waves. Felt the boiling moisture settle on his cheeks. It almost brought him out in sweats. Or maybe it was just because — as always — he was wearing his leather jacket indoors. The one emblazoned with the Swinton Rock 'n' Roll Brothas biker club patch across the spine. He'd started the Swinton Rock 'n' Roll Brothas with his best friend Phil back in '76. The club had come to an abrupt halt in '95 — just short of its twentieth year — when Phil had run out of road. He'd caught a heart attack at a marketing conference just outside Kettering. In a way, Gordon supposed that he continued to wear his jacket out of homage for Phil. To show his brother devil spawn, wherever he might be right now, that he would indeed continue to roll . . . albeit at a slower pace these days . . .

Gordon peered out through the grimy top-floor window of the Gorsing Community Centre, tucked away in the western reaches of the City of Brighton and Hove.

Storm clouds were building on the horizon. Rolling in over the English Channel. Fresh from France. Those clouds reminded Gordon of when his wife — Tabs — would leave cotton balls mottled with eyeshadow, and concealer, and who knew whatever else, on the bedside table. He thought of all the times, wrinkling his nose, he'd grabbed a handful of them and dumped them in the bin. Where they *should* be.

How times had changed . . . once upon a time *he'd* been the untidy one.

Even here, a good hundred yards or so from the beach, and with the window closed, he could smell the rain in the air. It would be piddling it down in half an hour. All that rubbish would trundle over here. Then it would pour down. Turn everything that grimy grey. Give it a good *soaking*. And him, like the lummox he was, had gone and left his umbrella at home.

He turned his attention away from the cheerful facades of the seafront homes — those *seaside* colours: sandy yellows, summer-sky blues, sunburn crimsons — all of them washed out by years of sun — years of salty air. He didn't dwindle for too long on the streets all inevitably slanting down to the beach, as if that was the place where all roads should naturally lead. It was difficult to get his head around the facts, most notable among them the one which declared that he'd been living here — in Brighton — for the best part of fifteen years. If back when he was in his twenties someone had asked him what he'd be doing when he was sixty-three — let alone *where* he'd be living — he'd have just laughed.

Wouldn't even have bothered to reply.

*Live fast, die young* . . . that old gem . . .

Well, he'd done his best to go out in a blaze and — sixty-three years later — he was still here. 'Live and kicking . . . though not *kicking* so much these days.

Over his shoulder, Gordon heard stamping feet. The echo of heavy boots carried through the wooden floorboards of the meeting room to the coffee pot here. He knew that passive-aggressive stamping anywhere. It'd be Margaret Maye — or 'Mistress M', as she went by in the back pages of the local rag, and in several dozen telephone booth advertisements. Seemed like he'd stepped out of the meeting at just the right time. He knew never to be in close proximity when the Mistress got to throwing her weight around.

Raised voices.

Check.

Screeching chair legs.

Check.

Quickening heartbeats.

Undoubtedly.

Once again, the excuse of 'putting on the coffee' was proven to be an unarguably successful strategy for the Vice-Chair of the Gorsing Neighbourhood Watch committee. When things began to get heated — like they had just now — he could simply rise up out of his seat and make for the coffee pot at the end of the corridor. Usually when he returned to the meeting things would have calmed down.

*Usually.*

Gordon was so lost in trying to discern just what those dampened voices said through the walls — just what vitriol was being tossed back and forth — that he nearly failed to notice that the coffee pot had filled. That the gooey, oil-black substance had spit forth into the glass chamber. To be quite honest, there was an argument to be had that a dose of caffeine wasn't likely to do anybody in that room any good. Graham himself wouldn't be indulging. His doctor had warded him off caffeine.

And stressful situations.

Gordon fished out the plastic bag containing the foam cups. He laid them out like soldiers on the table. As he slipped the coffee pot free from its place on the hot plate, he peered out of the window once more, down into the side alley.

Something caught his eye.

It was nothing more than a voice at the back of his skull — nagging him to take another look. Throughout the years he had learned to trust that little voice. More often than not, it steered him right. It had steered him in the direction of his wife, Tabs, after all. And, eyeshadow-soiled cotton balls aside, he had no room for complaints.

Realising he'd left his reading glasses on his chair back in the meeting room, he squinted, straining himself to better make out what was going on down in the alleyway.

It was a youth. About eighteen years old. Black hair slicked to his skull.

From the look of the blurry form, Gordon was certain that the youth was wearing a pair of overalls. And his mind naturally snapped onto the assumption that it must be a car mechanic. This assumption was soon replaced, however, when he realised what it was that the youth held in his hands. A pair of pliers.

Gordon absentmindedly allowed his hand to dangle. It came into contact with the near-scalding coffee pot. He restrained a curse. When he looked up again, cradling his hand to his beer belly, the youth was gone.

Coffee forgotten, he stumbled from the room.

---

As he loped along the corridor, the wrought-iron chain which hung from the pocket of his leather jacket to the belt loop of his black jeans chinked.

Usually the sound calmed him.

Like a secondary heartbeat.

Now, though, it proved more of a pain. He felt the chain pound against his thigh as he strode on. He had something of a permanent bruise right where the chain would strike him. His wife would often point it out to him. Tell him to stop wearing the chain . . . yeah, well, she'd been barking on about that for twenty-odd years now and wasn't getting anywhere.

The dozen or so people attending the Neighbourhood Watch meeting that evening were in varying poses when Gordon trod in through the doorway. He took in the Mistress right away. Purple. *Always* dressed in purple. Leather boots riding up to her thighs. Seeming almost to squeeze the fleshy parts of her calves up and over the sides. Like Gordon, she wore a leather jacket, but her jacket had been cropped so as to show off her bulging midriff while the leather had been buffed up to such a shine that Gordon fancied he could smell the polish cutting through the air.

As she stood hunched over a panicked-looking, blonde girl — university student? — Gordon found himself briefly hypnotised by her constantly jiggling Bingo wings. He supposed that was what folk paid good money for.

Ordinarily, Gordon would've followed the strategy of the others in the room, that of sitting about and watching on, in silence, waiting for the Mistress to blow herself out, but tonight he had justification for an interruption . . . other than on humanitarian grounds.

When he spoke, he was surprised at how easily his gruff voice cut over the Mistress's shrill tones. Perhaps this was the sort of authority the Vice-Chair of the Gorsing Neighbourhood Watch committee could command if he was just to put his back into it.

"The cables! They're after the cables!"

The whole room turned its attention away from the Mistress.

For a second, Gordon felt himself flush. He met with the stare of Ms Chambal, Chair of the Gorsing Neighbourhood Watch. Her grey-blue eyes — perfectly matched with the plaited hair she wore to the waist — crossed his. He felt a thrill in the pit of his stomach.

The theft of copper cabling had been an issue over the past year or so. To be quite honest, it was also an issue which was beyond the remit of the Watch. Then again, nobody signed up for the Neighbourhood Watch without at least an itch for danger.

A penchant for drama.

It was with this on his mind that Gordon turned his attention back to the scene and blurted out, "If we're quick we'll get 'em!"

Some people rose from their chairs.

Others — the majority — remained where they were.

In the once-a-month meetings they had with the local police force, the Watch was always 'discouraged' from taking matters into its own hands.

They needed to go through the *official* channels.

This was something which Nancy Mulligan, Treasurer, dressed — as always — in a smart navy-blue trouser suit with complimentary, brilliantly polished shoes, was very much in favour of. It was only when Reginald — *Redge* — Johnson, the Secretary, rocketed up from his seat and bounded for the door that the standoff truly ended. It was all Gordon could do to step to one side so he wouldn't be knocked onto his back.

Clearly realising that he had no idea where to head, Redge held back, pacing from side to side, his tracksuit trousers constantly slipping further and further down his legs as he did so. The gold chain about his neck glistened in the fluorescent lights of the corridor. A tiny Jamaican flag — flecked with silver — dangled from the chain.

"Where'd they go? Where'd you see them? What they grab?"

Gordon again shifted a glance back into the room, and to Ms Chambal and Nancy. He avoided meeting the Mistress's gaze. He saw that the two of them shared his concerns, and he knew that, as they always did, they acknowledged the unspoken truth.

It was a well-known fact that Redge had pretensions for becoming a policeman. Although Gordon went out of his way not to pry, he couldn't help but overhear the local gossip — usually filtered through his wife — that Redge had failed the copper exams more times than Gordon had flunked his driving test. Redge's dream was apparently unaffected, though. He still wanted to don the blue, or whatever colours police wore these days . . .

Trying to tell Redge that they were supposed to go through the 'official' channels was tantamount to kicking a new-born puppy in the face.

Realising he was going to have to act in *some* manner, Gordon turned his attention back to Redge. He looked over the kid's features. The enthusiasm. The will. The . . . *rage*?

Oh, what Gordon wouldn't do to feel those youthful passions again.

"In the alley. Alongside," Gordon finally replied, at the same time slipping Ms Chambal and Nancy a knowing look as he did so . . . and unable to keep himself from feeling that he'd just made some *grave* misstep.

---

Redge tore off through the Community Centre, apparently unwilling to wait on anybody. Gordon soon found himself reflecting on his own action — *inaction*? — when he fell into step with the Mistress. She cropped up at his elbow, speaking to him from out of the corner of her mouth in that *jawing* way of hers.

"Should see the damn state of my shrubs, Gordo. Some people've got a nerve's all I'll say. Get in at blinkin' a clock, with blinkin'-knows-who, and they get to neckin' against *my* bushes." She shook her head, sending waves of loose skin bouncing up and down from her throat. "Don't bother me, mind you, none of them *personal* things bother me . . ."

Gordon thought — considering the Mistress's choice of occupation — that was only fair. And, to tell the truth, he supposed that the Mistress had more of an alibi than the average curtain twitcher. She *did* keep a nocturnal schedule after all. Her work *demanded* it.

"It's just . . . it's just . . ." The Mistress seemed to become exasperated, and Gordon noticed her padding the breast pockets of her jacket. He knew what question would be coming next. She eyed him with those fierce green irises of hers and puckered her lips. "Got a cigarette, love?"

"'Fraid not," Gordon replied. "Quit smoking . . . twenty years ago."

The Mistress eyeballed him a fraction of a second longer, then her mouth turned at the corners. For the shortest of moments Gordon was convinced that she was going to scratch his eyes out. Then she broke into a full-on smile. She slapped her forehead with her palm. "Jesus, Mary and Joseph," she said. "*My* memory, eh?"

"Yeah," Gordon replied, realising that they were leaving the Community Centre now, venturing out into the cool late-evening sea air.

Outside, a light drizzle was falling. He popped the collar of his leather jacket and peered from side to side.

No sign of the youth in overalls.

And no sign of Redge either.

When Redge had first started coming to the meetings, Gordon had felt some sort of a paternal affection for the boy. He had wanted to 'take him under his wing', or some crap like that. It had soon transpired, of course, that Redge wasn't in need of any wing. He could fend for himself just fine. Gordon could still recall the meeting where they had held the vote for the posts within the Watch. And he could easily bring to mind the expression which'd crossed Redge's face when Ms Chambal — for the umpteenth time — had been re-elected to the role of Chair while Redge had had to settle for the consolation prize of Secretary.

Redge had had the good sense not to say anything at all, but Gordon had noted how he'd bunched his fists down at his sides, and how his eyes had narrowed. How he'd muttered something or other underneath his breath.

No, Gordon had soon decided that it wasn't Redge at all who was in need of protection, but those who Redge *pursued.*

Gordon did his best to pull away from the Mistress, wanting, if at all possible, to put more distance between him and her. But he had no luck. As he plodded on harder, turning the corner, again squinting to bring the blurry streetscape straight, he felt the Mistress literally breathing down his neck.

"What's that?" the Mistress said, pointing. "Over there?"

Gordon squinted. He followed her purple-painted fingernail. And saw nothing but a collection of blurry, seemingly formless shapes. He took a second to separate them, at least superficially.

Curb.

Streetlamp.

Rubbish bin.

When he blinked again, he realised what it was that the Mistress was indicating. But she was already striding in the direction of the form.

He plodded along behind.

She stooped to retrieve the item.

Pliers.

Gordon followed the Mistress's gaze, seeing that she was

looking off down a nearby side alley. Again, the incoming darkness got the better of him and it was only by squinting that he was able to make out the pair of forms there. He realised that Redge was staring back at him, over his shoulder, grinning from ear to ear.

And that Redge was sitting on top of someone.

"Got 'im!" Redge declared, with true glee in his voice.

Gordon slipped a glance to the Mistress, and he half fixed his thoughts on the eventuality of her pulling some handcuffs from somewhere about her person. He was sure that if any one member of the Watch *possessed* a pair of handcuffs then it would be the Mistress. However, the Mistress was strangely bashful now . . . for want of a better term.

She seemed unwilling to close the gap.

To throw herself into the jaws of unknown danger.

Gordon, though, being a career motorcyclist, had no such qualms.

Hearing the remnants of the Watch following close behind, he stepped up to Redge, and looked down on the boy who he sat upon. "What's he got, then?" Gordon asked.

Redge looked a touch bemused. "I . . . dunno," he replied.

Seeing the complexion of the man Redge sat on had turned puce, Gordon said, "Let off a bit, I reckon."

Redge remained where he was, clearly unwilling to give the suspect a chance to bolt for escape. Finally, he relented. The two of them stood over the downed figure. Neither one of them spoke for a long time. From the way the man lay still, Gordon managed to convince himself Redge had accidently killed him . . . or at least rendered him unconscious.

However, with an understandably reluctant lifting of his head, the man looked about.

And then up.

Even without his glasses to hand, Gordon could see right away where he'd gone wrong; that they hadn't been dealing with a 'he' at all. That this was a *she*.

Slowly looking around at the rapidly assembling members of the Neighbourhood Watch at the entrance to the alleyway, the girl found her feet. She looked them over. Blunt surprise had given way to a skittishness which had settled in over her expression.

"I . . . what . . . what is this?" she said.

Gordon crossed his arms over his chest. He was deeply aware of the Mistress standing beside him, and of Ms Chambal and Nancy Mulligan over his shoulder, keeping an eye on every one of the suspect's movements. "Where are they?" he asked. "You toss them?"

The girl — who Gordon now noticed had red hair and fragile, doll-like features — looked to the many faces spectating before shifting her attention back to him. "Toss *what*?"

"The cables."

"I . . ." The girl shook her head. "What're you *talking* about?"

Beginning to feel uneasy, and getting a sinking sense in his stomach, Gordon glanced about the alleyway, wondering if she was an extraordinarily good actor.

Or if there was some other reason.

When Gordon spoke again, he realised his gruff voice didn't carry any of the authority it had before. Or which he had *imagined* it had carried before.

"I saw you," he said. "From up there." He pointed in the general direction of the Gorsing Community Centre as if this would aid understanding.

The girl continued to stand still. She looked about the other members of the Gorsing Neighbourhood Watch, and then turned back to Gordon. "Listen," she said, "if anyone's been wronged here then it's surely me." She shook her head. "I was just minding my business, coming home from the studio where I was working on my end-of-year project. A *sculpture*."

Looking at her now, in the overalls, Gordon realised that there was a daubing of plaster dust clinging to the material.

"And then," she continued, jerking her thumb in Redge's direction, "out of *nowhere*, he grabs a hold of me . . . I break free . . . then he chases me down this alleyway and jumps on top of me." Her eyes widened now and — for the first time — a fierceness entered her expression. "Just who do you think you are? Some sort of vigilante justice? What makes you think you can go around *chasing* people?"

Gordon allowed her words to sink in. He could feel everyone's stare upon him. He knew that this was all his fault. That this had *been* all his fault. He was the one who had to own up to this, give the girl the explanation she so surely deserved.

"We're not vigilantes," he said, "we're the Gorsing Neighbourhood Watch."

He thought for a second, feeling himself begin to blush. He always believed that it must look somewhat surreal for an observer to see a man in his sixties, dressed in a leather motorcycle jacket, with a bushy black beard blushing. And yet, there it was . . .

Strangely, the first thing which came to him was the tagline they had come up with in the past year; the one which adorned all the stationary and the various signs hanging up throughout the neighbourhood. "We go beyond the blinds," he said.

The girl flared her nostrils, tossed her head, then sighed. She rolled her eyes, and then strode past Gordon. As she disappeared from view, Gordon was certain that he heard her mutter, under her breath, "Bloody curtain twitchers."

Even if he'd had the chance of replying, he didn't know what he might've said.

Because she was right.

How had Gordon ended up like this? How had his life led him to *this* point? What did *he* care what went on in his neighbourhood?

"Well," the Mistress said, finally breaking the silence which hung over the side alley, "I'm looking forward to a good, hot cup of coffee after that."

Gordon felt a pang in his stomach to think of the forgotten coffee pot. And it was a good excuse for him to break free of the group and hot foot it back to the Community Centre. As he went, he couldn't help but overhear the Mistress starting into her complaints with her neighbour once again. Gordon supposed it was just going to be one of *those* meetings. It was all part and parcel of keeping the community safe.

Or something like that . . .

# Through The Oval Window

With a sudden, violent breath, I stirred.

My eyes wrenched open.

The world blurred in front of me.

Night-time.

Streetlight bled in through undrawn curtains.

Silence — *stillness* — everywhere.

I was in the front hall of my home. The place where I had bid my nurse farewell. Where she had left me in my wheelchair to soak up the pain. I could still recall the pitying half-smile she had given me as she had slipped out of the door.

She would do more if she could.

I knew that.

Everybody said so without saying it out loud. There was nothing to be done with such an unfortunate situation, except to give me the time and space I required.

To die.

I stretched my nostrils, half expecting to breathe in the stringent odour of urine. It wouldn't have been the first time. But it might well have been the last time. My sense of smell had almost completely deserted me, and it seemed a curse that I could still so easily recognise my own distinctive stench.

Outside, I could hear a breeze fluttering the leaves of the trees.

I looked up to the oval window, seeing down my garden path, to the street outside. And to the houses which stood in a row. All of them with their curtains drawn. No warm lights shining out from within. Their occupants clearly sleeping. Preparing for the merry summer's day which would surely follow in this chain of perfect weather. And the world went on, as I slumped in my wheelchair — just trying to live with the pain.

For what reason even *I* didn't truly know any longer.

My breathing made an impossible cacophony. There was the hissing drawl as the air passed through my nostrils, and then the rasping choke as it made its way down my throat — finally, there was the inevitable rattle in my chest, which never failed to cause my whole body to quiver. And then the process began again.

But even through this discordant symphony, I could hear something.

Something outside.

More than just the breeze.

More than mere elements.

*People.*

One half of my face was alive with an uncontrollable twitching, and although I felt unbelievably exhausted, I knew I would sleep no more tonight.

I knew I had had what rest I could hope for.

All I had to look forward to now was the mercifully short wait for sunrise. That grapefruit tinge flaming the corners of the world. And for my nurse's courteous knock at the door. And for her pitying look — a slight disappointment as I read it — that I wasn't yet dead. That I was still hanging on.

Hands trembling, I reached down for the wheels of my chair, pirouetting with perhaps too much grace for a condemned man. One of the last kindnesses I had been afforded by a brother — or had it been a sister — was the linoleum floor which'd been set across the carpet of my home so as to ease my wheelchair's progress.

I rolled into my kitchen, and found myself looking out through the window.

Into my back garden.

It was something like a riot out there in the moonlight, with the alien, mauvish-blues of the delphiniums sprouting tall and wild and unwieldy; the godetia enflamed blushes which wouldn't go away; and the roses, with their jagged, cutting thorns drawing blood just as easily as any needle.

Sometimes I would sit slumped in my wheelchair — was there any other way for me to sit — and stare out into the back garden all night. I would see the hedgehogs rooting back and forth across the lawn. And watch the darting progress of the odd field mouse through the long grasses (it was weeks since the lawn had last been mown by a well-meaning nephew).

But there was something more, tonight.

Something which didn't fit.

And I could see this something — this *someone* — pressed up against the garden fence.

All dressed in black, and clearly believing such a trick might make him invisible.

I said nothing — only stared.

And I believed he stared back at me.

Our eyes meeting in the darkness.

Perhaps it was minutes — maybe it was hours — but it was he who made the first move. He peeled away from the garden fence, approaching the back door with a prowling gait. Like a cat which fools only itself that it is acting in a sly manner — that it has yet to be detected by either its prey or its chaperone.

When he peered in through the glass, I felt myself slipping into his bottomless black eyes. He wore a balaclava which exposed only the oval slit across his eyes. He reached for the doorknob and I heard the familiar rattle as it stirred in its housing. I had been meaning to fix that the very same day I had been admitted to hospital. The very same day when my life had become a husk . . . when I had suddenly become so very *delicate.*

It surprised me that there was no lock on the door, that this intruder had only to turn the handle and to step over the threshold. I thought about all the neighbourhood watch meetings I had attended over the years, about how the list of phone numbers which had been shared throughout the neighbourhood was still stuck to my fridge with an Eifel Tower magnet. That I had only to wheel myself back — to surprise this man with my nimbleness — and to snatch the cordless phone from its cradle.

To dial.

To speak.

To wait.

But nothing really mattered any longer.

Once he had stepped into the kitchen, he brought the door shut behind him. He glanced about, as if there might be someone other than me there. When his eyes fell upon mine again, he reached for the base of his balaclava and yanked it up and over his head.

Wild, stringy blond hair bounced down to his shoulders.

A golden earring sparkled.

Even in the half-light of the moon, I could see he had a scar just above his left eyebrow. There was no need for any light at all to see he was grinning.

"You all alone, old man?" he asked, his voice husky, almost on the brink of laughter.

"I'm not as old as you think."

The man looked about me, taking inventory of my kitchen with a kind of professional efficiency. He was much younger than I had first believed — maybe no more than eighteen, nineteen. A boy? I supposed that I probably *was* what qualified as old to him.

"There anyone else in the house?" he asked, reaching into his jacket, and withdrawing some object.

"Not that I know of."

The boy's smile faded as he eyed the object in his hand. Moonlight fell upon the edge of the blade. A knife. He looked to me. "You gonna be quiet, right? Not gonna have problems?"

"Right."

"To tell the truth you scared me half to death."

"I'm terribly sorry to hear that."

Holding the knife down at his side, he made a comb of his fingers and swept back his hair. He glanced out into the back garden. "Thought you were already dead, see? Thought they'd taken your body away, and all. When I saw you from out there" — here he brought his knife up and tapped the blade against the window pane, making a glassy *clink-clink* sound — "I thought I might be seeing a ghost, or whatever."

"What made you think I was dead?"

"Well, nobody's been round much recently. Haven't seen you at the front door."

"You obviously haven't seen my nurse."

A smirk twitched the boy's lips. "Yeah, must've missed her. More fool me, huh?"

My whole body was stiff with tension, and I realised I was still gripping tightly to the wheels of my chair, as if I might be able to make a human battering ram of myself — as if I might be able to propel my body at his kneecaps, knock him to the ground.

*Run him over.*

But I felt nothing.

No animosity.

No kindness, either, though.

"Must be glad for the company," the boy said, treading about the kitchen, pausing to inspect the odd item of possible value — a silver pocket watch which'd belonged to my grandfather; a glittering elephant which appeared to be entirely made up of diamonds; an emerald pair of dice which a brother had brought back by way of a souvenir from Las Vegas. "Don't 'spose you get much people round, anymore." Apparently unmoved by the items he had thus far seen, he tilted his head back and yawned. "I remember when my nanna started to go — you know, when she was hanging on for a year, or whatever — people started to get bored of visiting her. Waiting for her to drop. Not me, though. I didn't get bored with it. I went to go see her every day."

The insistence with which the boy made this statement put me on edge. And it did nothing to push his case, either. It made it seem as if he was compensating for something . . . not that I was going to inflame him by saying otherwise.

"Where's the telly?" the boy asked, glancing in the direction of the front hall.

"Through there, on your right."

The boy nodded, still holding the knife down at his side. He stole through the darkness, slipping from my vision. I eyed the phone, on the hook, and wondered if I had the strength to call for help.

What would be the point?

In the silent house, the boy would easily hear my shaky voice. He would be long gone with whatever he wished to take with him before any sort of help arrived.

I remained where I was, parked in my wheelchair, watching, waiting to see what would happen next.

The boy returned from the sitting room. "Load of old shit,

that thing," he said. "Dunno how you've got on for so long with such a tiny screen."

"I don't tend to watch much television."

"No, don't 'spose I would either with a screen like that." The boy snorted phlegm up his nose, then glanced about the kitchen once more. "You not got nothing worth nicking, or what?"

I had no idea how to answer the question — or whether I was even *supposed* to answer the question. So I remained still.

Silent.

The boy exhaled strongly, blowing hair free from his mouth. He disappeared upstairs, taking little trouble to make his steps light as he went.

I listened to him rooting about in the upstairs rooms — first venturing through the spare room, before going onto my bedroom. I created a mental picture of him, looking through the chests of drawers, and finding nothing of much material value.

I turned my attention to the back garden — to the place I had spent so much of my time. I looked to all the twisting, turning plants sprouting from the flowerbeds, and wondered whether it hadn't been a tremendous waste of time.

But then, what else might I have spent my time on?

Outside, there was the sound of a car engine approaching. I turned my head and looked into the front hall. I peered through the oval window above the door, seeing the car pulling up to the curb outside. The car itself was inconspicuous — a family hatchback. It was impossible to make out the driver in the darkness, but why would I have wanted to do that?

Upstairs, I heard an enormous *thud* followed by a series of swearwords.

I suppose that he had perhaps tried to get a better look at the cricket bat I had mounted on my bedroom wall, only to have it drop at his feet. Perhaps under other circumstances, I might've wished that it had clubbed his big toe — given him a great, big bruise — but I decided that I just didn't care either way.

I felt no animosity towards the boy.

Soon I would be gone.

I listened to the boy's progress overhead. He plodded his way down the stairs. When he emerged in the hallway once again, he pinned his gaze to the oval window and swore another time — apparently seeing the car waiting outside.

He turned back to me. "Christ, man, you really have nothing — nothing at all, do you?"

I remained silent.

"Not even got nobody here with you." A hint of unease had entered the boy's voice. His throat constricted about his vocal chords. "Why've you got nothing, huh? What're you trying to do?"

"I'm not trying to *do* anything."

The boy's eyes flared. He leaned over me, close to my face. His breath stank of warm onions. He held the knife blade to the corner of my eyeball and pressed it lightly into my papery skin. "Maybe I should just cut you and be done with it."

I said nothing.

"You ready to die, pal?"

". . . Yes."

The boy continued to stare into my eyes. His stare was cold, unfeeling. The knife didn't shake in his grip. My skin might have torn, but I didn't feel it, and no blood dribbled down my face. Finally, the boy blinked, breaking the gaze which locked the two of us together. He straightened up, sheathing the knife. He shifted around, looked through the oval window, to the car outside. "I'll be back, you know? Don't believe there's nothing here. Maybe I'll have the chance to look properly when you're gone."

"Yes, maybe."

The boy nodded to himself, and then snorted through his nostrils again. Then — without another word — he unlatched the front door, trod over the step, and disappeared up the garden path to the waiting car. I watched on as he rounded the car, got into the passenger seat, and then drove off with his accomplice, leaving me alone.

The sweet night air drifted in through the open front door.

I remained where I was for the longest time, peering into the silent street — into the sleeping world — and then, deciding that I might as well uphold some sense of order, even amongst my darkest hours, I wheeled over to the front door and closed it.

Sealing everybody out.

And myself in.

# Author's Note

Thank you for taking the time to read one of my books. If you would like to hear about my latest releases you can sign up for my newsletter here: www.aviain.com

Thanks for reading!

*AV Iain*

**Killing Time**
**A Short Story Collection**


Published by DIB Books, 2018.

www.ingramcontent.com/pod-product-compliance
Lightning Source LLC
Chambersburg PA
CBHW031214260626
47169CB00007B/2051

* 9 7 8 1 7 8 5 3 2 0 6 5 1 *